The Sisterhood

Anthony Weedon

AuthorHouse™ UK Ltd.
500 Avebury Boulevard
Central Milton Keynes, MK9 2BE
www.authorhouse.co.uk
Phone: 08001974150

© 2009 Anthony Weedon. All rights reserved.

No part of this book may be reproduced, stored in a retrieval system, or transmitted by any means without the written permission of the author.

First published by AuthorHouse 9/10/2009

ISBN: 978-1-4389-9240-2 (sc)

This book is printed on acid-free paper.

For Maureen

Chapter 1

Faith

Looking back on his long life, Roy had few regrets. Although he had always lived in the same place and travelled very little, he knew more of the world than most of those who had travelled all over it, and the reason for this could be summed up in one word: women. At least, that's how he saw it, and there had been five of them; that's to say, five that really counted; and it had all begun with Faith, who was a headmistress and old enough to be his mother.

Now retired, Roy had left school at fourteen in 1944 to work in the gardens at Ashden Hall, where he had worked his way up to the position of head gardener well before he was thirty. Roy's father had been the local wheelwright, a business that he had inherited from his father. It had since been taken over by Roy's only and much older half-brother Fred, who had turned it into a carpentry and cabinet making enterprise to suit changing circumstances. Since Roy had shown an aptitude for working with wood, Fred had wanted him to become a partner in the business, but Roy wouldn't hear of it. Having absorbed a love of gardening from his father, who practised it as a relaxation from wheelwrighting, he had made an early decision to make it his life's work, not least because he didn't fancy working with the domineering Fred.

Lord Denver, who owned Ashden Hall, had contrived to have Roy employed as a farm worker by including pig feeding in his duties. This was because he did not want his training to be interrupted by his having to do national service in one of the armed forces. Whereas farm workers were exempt from national service in the armed forces, gardeners were not. Lord Denver, who was descended from a baron who had come to England with William the Conqueror, did not believe in mixing trades. Soldiering was soldiering and gardening was gardening, and he saw no point in muddling them together, and he was concerned that the call up of young men for national service would continue long after the war with Germany, which he now believed to be in its final stages.

Fred's mother having died soon after he was born, William, his father had contrived to wed Mary, his sixteen year old housemaid, who had taken over the mothering of the infant as if it were her own. Fifteen years later, at the age of thirty one, after she had given up any hope of ever having a child, Mary gave birth to Roy; but, try as she might, hoping for a baby girl, there were no more. William wasn't at all bothered. Reasoning that two children were easier to provide for than three, he was inwardly relieved that frequent intercourse with his attractive little, brown eyed second wife had failed to produce more results.

Roy was exceptional in that he was both a father's and a mother's boy. Mild mannered, he enjoyed both indoor and outdoor activities. Brought up in the midst of a rolling, Constable-style, Suffolk landscape, he found it difficult to distinguish between playtime and work-time. He played to learn how to work, and he worked as if he were playing. Even at school he juggled around with letters, and then words and figures, as if he were playing a game. Mary's mother, who lived nearby, was concerned that the boy was missing out on his childhood, but Mary knew better. 'All life's a joy to him,' she would say. 'And one day he'll make some lucky woman a good husband.' Little did she know than that Roy would do more than that - much more; and it all began with Faith.

It was Boxing Day 1946 and Roy had been invited to tea at Kiln Cottage where Faith lived with her older sister Charity, but he couldn't for the life of him think why. Faith had never taught him. He had gone to the village school in Ashden, whereas she taught three miles away at Teddlethwaite school and he didn't really know that much about her or her sister, except that neither of them were married and that Charity kept house while Faith taught. Their mother had died many years ago and their father had passed away just before the outbreak of war. Before he retired in 1938, he had made bricks at the local, now redundant, kiln. Hence the name of the cottage. Faith was organist at Saint Mary's Church in the village and Charity taught in the Sunday School. Their mother, a devout Christian, had chosen the girls' names as precursors of the high moral standards she would expect of her offspring as they grew up.

Having read the carefully crafted invitation from the sisters, Roy looked askance at his mother Mary. 'Must I go?'

Mary nodded. 'I think you should. After all, it's only afternoon tea. You could be back home again soon after six.'

'But why me? They hardly know me.'

'Your father and theirs were great friends. And there's something else…'

'What's that?'

'Gardening. Charity is a keen gardener. She may be wanting you to filch her a cutting or two from the hall gardens.'

'John Lankester's the head gardener. Why doesn't she ask him?'

'I don't know. Maybe she wants to encourage you. You know she always takes a keen interest in anyone she taught at Sunday School, and not long ago I was telling her how well you were getting along at the Hall.'

Roy sighed. 'Oh, very well the, I suppose I'd best go.'

Roy took the short cut to Kiln Cottage across the deer park, on through Badgers' Wood and out onto Kiln Lane passed the disused brick kiln and up to the front door of Kiln House. On the look out for him, Faith came to the front gate to meet him and took him inside to where Charity was lighting the lamps. Taking hold of one of them, Faith led the way into the front sitting room where a log fire was blazing away in the large fireplace.

'Tea's in the other room,' she said. 'Charity will call us when it's ready. I'm so glad you could come.' She bade him sit down in a low arm chair on the far side of the hearth from where she presently seated herself in a much higher, hard backed chair.

Used to his mother's petite neatness, Roy found himself disconcerted by this woman's buxom presence, a voluptuosity that was actually more apparent than real, it having as much to do with the way she was dressed as it had with her actual figure. Her dress, of a flimsy, flowered variety, seemed all wrong for a chilly winter's day and it was rather on the short side, a fact that became all too apparent when she crossed her legs. Suspecting that, from his lower position, he might well be able to see up to her stocking tops, Roy tried hard to keep his gaze fixed on her face as she began talking to him. Her straight, brown hair, just long enough to cover her ears, hugged her face in a quite becoming fashion so as to emphasise the fullness of her bright red lips beneath an invitingly turned up nose. There was a sauciness about her that made her more attractive than a more classically beautiful woman might have been. However, there was no play acting here. Faith wasn't trying to create any kind of impression, and Roy had the distinct feeling that he was seeing the woman as she actually was.

'I hope you don't mind my sitting up here,' she was saying. 'The fact is, I always prefer a hard chair, and this one's my favourite. Now, the sofa, that's different; I don't mind a good stretch out on that; but that's also what Charity likes to do; so I leave it to her. To tell the truth, I like to get stripped off early on these cold winter evenings and get to bed where I can snuggle up with a good book.'

Startled by the abruptness of the phrase 'stripped off' where one might have expected to hear 'undressed', Roy was in for a second shock as he lowered his gaze in a futile attempt to hide his embarrassment. The flimsy dress had ridden up that much further to reveal a suspender with its attendant expanse of bare thigh. What was this woman playing at? As if by instinct, he knew the answer to that question right away: nothing. She was following her normal pattern of relaxed behaviour within the haven our her own home.

Suddenly, he blurted out: 'Oughtn't you to wear a warmer dress on a cold day like this?'

Faith giggled. 'My! What a direct young man you are!'

'I'm sorry… I didn't mean…'

'Oh, that's all right, I know you didn't, and I don't mind a bit. The fact is, it gets hot in here of an evening with the big open fire. If we're on our own I often change into my nightdress early and wear a dressing gown, but since we have a visitor, I though a pretty dress would be more appropriate. Do you like it?'

'Oh yes, very much,' Roy responded quickly, but it wasn't the dress he was liking so much as the sturdy thigh its meagre length had contrived to reveal.

Just then, relief came in the form of Charity. Roy stood up as she entered the room. Bidding him sit down, she flashed him an unexpectedly bright smile as she sat down on the sofa, telling him that he was quite the gentleman.

Roy blushed as he sat down and turn to look in her direction. She was dressed in a bright blue, close fitting jumper that matched the colour of her eyes and she wore a string of pearls to match her earrings. Her calf-length, beige coloured skirt covered her knees and she didn't cross her shapely legs, which were clad in warm looking, country style stockings. Her hair was fairer than her sisters, verging on blond, shoulder length and carefully coiffured, and her neat features lacked both her sisters full lips and her excessively tilted nose. Turning his gaze back towards Faith, he noticed that she had now crossed her legs the other way, granting him a view of her other thigh. Then, as he raised his gaze, he wondered why, unlike her sister, she was wearing no jewellery.

'You like my sister's outfit?' she said.

Roy nodded. 'Yes, indeed; it's very neat.'

'Well, that's Charity: always the neat one. As for me, I'm afraid all my neatness goes on running the school.'

Charity chuckled. 'That's why we forgive her for not being tidy at home.'

Roy watched as Faith re-crossed her legs for the second time, causing her flimsy dress to ride up another inch or so to reveal even more of her sturdy thighs above her stocking tops. She asked him if he still enjoyed gardening. When he replied that he certainly did, especially growing vegetables, she told him that perhaps he would care to visit Charity now and then give her some advice about her small vegetable patch.

'Yes, indeed,' said Charity. 'That's really why we invited you here. If you could spare any time, we thought you might like to come and do the digging for us. We'd pay you well, of course.'

Roy hesitated. 'Well… I would, except that it's getting the time. I do get time off, of course, but not that much, and what I do get is used up mostly with woodworking and violin practice.'

The sisters had heard about his skill with the violin. Faith asked if he played at any dances.

Roy nodded. 'Yes, indeed; but I'm not too keen on that. You see, if I'm playing, I don't get to dance, and I like dancing.'

Wanting to know what kind of dancing he preferred, Charity was delighted to learn that he like waltzing. 'But isn't that somewhat old fashioned for someone of your age?'

Roy agreed. 'Yes it is; but you see, it was the war. We couldn't get out so much then and mother taught me how to dance in all kinds of ways; but she doesn't know any of the modern ones.'

Faith wanted to know if he liked folk dancing. He certainly did, and he would also like to learn Morris dancing. 'They've recently reformed a Morris dancing team near Ipswich,' he said. 'But it's too far away for me to join.'

Charity told him that Faith was thinking of buying a car. 'It's not so easy for her bringing school things to and fro on her bicycle,' she said. 'So, if you come and dig our vegetable garden, she might agree to drive you to the classes.'

Voicing his approval of this proposal, Roy also bore in mind that Faith might even be persuaded to teach him how to drive. 'I'll be seventeen in March,' he said.

Faith giggled. 'Decent of you to tell us your age. Easy for a man to do so, but not for a woman, they say. But the two of us don't mind. I'm thirty eight and Charity is forty two.'

Roy looked straight at Charity. 'You look much younger than that,' he said.

Faith feigned disappointment. 'What about me? Are you going to tell me I look **forty** eight or something?'

Bringing her sturdy thighs into his line of sight again, Roy shook his head. 'I suppose I feel I have to treat you with extra respect on account of your being a headmistress,' he said.

'Nice of you to say so; but here when I'm off duty at home, I like to relax and be seen as… as…'

'Just a woman?' Roy suggested.

Faith nodded. 'What an understanding boy you are,' she said in a decidedly wistful tone of voice.

Later, over tea in the dining room, they discussed church matters. Charity wanted to know why Roy had stopped attending church. Not wishing to distress her by saying he no longer believed that there any such thing as God, he hedged. Sensing his difficulty, Faith came to the rescue, saying it was the music that kept her going to church. 'Charity takes after mother,' she added. 'For her, Christianity is a way of life. For me, it's the music. She's for the stem and I'm for the offshoot, if you see what I mean. Or to put it another way, music is a fruit of religion.'

After tea they returned to the sitting room, where Charity got Roy to help her move some of the furniture. 'I'll get Faith to play the piano so as we can dance,' she said.

She was delighted with Roy's performance as Faith played through a repertoire of different kinds of dance. After the lapse of half an hour or so, Roy suggested that Charity played the piano to give Faith a chance to dance, but Charity shook her head. She couldn't play any musical instrument. So Faith began playing again and Roy had to be content with Charity for another half hour. After that, Roy thought he had better be getting home. Charity was reluctant to let him go, but Faith didn't seem to mind, and Roy was surprised when she suggested that Charity went and got on with the washing up whilst she fetched his coat and saw him off.

Following Charity into the hall, Roy was surprised when she suddenly exclaimed: 'Stop right there!'

Halting in his tracks, he glanced around him. Faith chuckled. 'You haven't seen it, have you?'

Looking up, Roy was just in time to see the sprig of mistletoe as Faith closed in on him and pressed his back against the wall and her lips to his. Then, as he hesitated, not knowing how to react, she bade him in husky tones, to open his mouth and place his arms around her. Not knowing what else to do, he obeyed. Then, as her lips parted, and he made contact with the inside of her mouth, he realised that this is what he had been wanting to do all evening. After a few moments, she disconnected and held her face from him to look into his eyes, telling him how blue they were.

'And yours are green,' he said.

'Hazel green,' she corrected before connecting her mouth to his again.

This time there was no holding back. He couldn't get enough of her. It was if they were trying to eat each other, and how sweet it tasted! Maybe God didn't exist, but heaven certainly did because the two of them were in it. Thrilling to the firm rotundity of her ample buttocks as he felt them with his hands, he presently made contact with her suspenders through her thin dress as he explored downwards.

Disconnecting for a moment, Faith whispered; 'You like my thighs, don't you?'

'Yes, I do. Did you want me to see them?'

Faith nodded before uniting her mouth to his yet again, this time for an even longer kiss, during which Roy contrived to lift her dress from behind enabling him to feel the naked flesh of her thighs and lower buttocks, an action that caused him an exhilaration passing even that of dancing over a rolling green landscape on a bright spring day. Immersed thus in their freshly created heaven, they barely heard the click of the door handle that heralded Charity's emergence from the kitchen. She must have seen everything, not least the lifted dress and Roy's hand clasping her sister's buttocks, but she said nothing as the two of them parted and turned towards her. Faith pointed upwards at the mistletoe as she searched for the right words to cover the situation.

Charity forestalled her with a wave of the hand. 'Best let the boy go now. They'll be wondering where he's got to.' Fetching Roy's overcoat from the peg, she held it out for him. Slipping into it as if in a dream, he took his hat, scarf and gloves from her and stepped out into the crisp coldness of the star studded night.

'You must come and see us again!' Faith called after.

Pausing, he turned to look back at her, nodding his head as he did so.

'Yes, please do! Any time!' Charity's tone of voice was decisive.

After he had gone, the sisters stood in the hall looking at each other for several moments. Faith was the first to speak. 'Do you think he'll ever come back to see us?' she said.

Charity's nod was decisive. 'Oh yes, he certainly will. It may take some time, but one day he'll be back and that's for sure.'

Still not entirely convinced, Faith moved to return to the

sitting room. She was thinking of lovers. She'd had several of them, men she had used, and regarded with some contempt. She'd led them all up the garden path, just using them. She wasn't the marrying kind. But Charity, she was different, and she blamed herself for the fact that her sister had never married. So what now? Neither of them would marry, and she was reduced to playing with boys; but what a boy this one was! There was potential here all right, and she wished her age would stand still while he grew up towards her. Turning to look at Charity, who had followed her into the room, she said suddenly: 'I think I've fallen in love.'

Charity flashed her a devastating look. 'In love! You in love! Don't talk like a bloody fool!' She rarely swore, reserving her 'bloodies' to emphasise her greatest contempt.

Meanwhile, Roy was on his way home through the copse and out into the deer park. At the churchyard he paused to watch as the ghostly whiteness of a barn owl glided among the tombstones. Then, as it disappeared behind the church, he too entered in among them, fearless, for he was not afraid of the dead. Soon he was home and, after playing his violin for a while, he turned in for an early night. Although he slept soundly for some time, in the early hours he began to dream. He was in a vast forest standing before two great boulders of equal size, the rotundity of which amazed him. Where the roundness of them curved away from each other, he espied an entrance. Crawling on his hands and knees, he found himself in a narrow passage at the end of which he espied a bright light. Wriggly along towards it, he soon found himself within a brightly lit cavern where a beautiful girl in a tight fitting short dress was dancing. He watched, spellbound, as the dress split open and she wriggled towards him, he reached out with his hands to clasp her buttocks and draw her to him as she presented a pink-nippled breast for him to suck. A feeling of immense joy enveloped him, followed by a tremendous thrill as he awoke to find he had ejaculated into his pyjamas. He lay there savouring the experience for a while, before whispering, 'Thank you Faith,' and drifted back into a contented sleep.

Chapter 2

Sisters

The following day, Roy went to work at Ashden Hall Gardens as if nothing untoward had happened on the day before. Glad to be out in the crisp, cold air in the bright but weak sunlight, he worked happily away at a tidying up job in one of the shrubberies. Since he was making good progress in learning all kinds of gardening skills, he was happy to do his fair share of the chores. As he worked on and his mind flashed back to the events of the previous evening, he didn't think he would be in a hurry to visit Faith and Charity again, if ever. Although he had all the natural male feelings about women and girls, he mostly gave them a wide berth, preferring to dream now and then of ideals rather than to dabble in disappointing realities. In any case, his greatest love was the village, and he never wanted to leave it. Goodness knows what some woman or other might want him to do, and he was prepared to wait for the right one who wouldn't want him to go and live somewhere else. What Faith had been up to, he couldn't be entirely sure. Fair enough, she was a village girl and never likely to live anywhere else, but she was old enough to be his mother. Perhaps she just wanted to be good friends. He was all for friendship. He would have to wait and see how things turned out.

Later that January it was the weather that decided his fate. It had been freezing hard and, when the snow came on an easterly wind, it was blown into deep drifts that blocked roads all around the village. Banding together, the villagers began clearing the snow in an effort to renew contact with the outside world. Little did they know then that the snow and ice would not be finally gone until early April. The great lake in the deer park froze feet thick and everyone wanted to skate on it. However, as few had any skates, most contented themselves with tobogganing down the steep sloop at the west side of the park, having either made their own sleds or paid Roy's brother Fred to make some for them at the wheelwright's yard.

It was early March before Roy saw Faith again. It was Saturday morning and he was returning from having helped to clear a fresh drift of snow near the post office when he met her cycling into village. Dismounting, she waited for him to draw close before addressing him with: 'Long time no see.'

Roy apologised. 'It's the weather. There's a lot to see to up at the hall and extra work everywhere with all these drifts to clear.'

Faith's green eyes twinkled. 'And the skating. I hear you've been doing a lot of it recently.'

Roy nodded. 'It's good fun by moonlight,' he said.

A saucy smile crinkled around the enticing fullness of Faith's red lips. 'There's a full moon tonight,' she said.

Looking up at the sky, Roy said: 'That's right, but it'll be no use unless the clouds clear.'

Faith adopted a confident tone. 'They will, they certainly

will; and we're in for another hard frost I shouldn't wonder. So how about you and I going skating together in the moonlight.'

Roy shook his head. 'I don't think that would be a good idea.'

'But, why ever not?'

'Well... You're a headmistress and a respected lady in the village.'

'Headmistress? Senior teacher in a two teacher school, more like. As for 'respected lady' - fiddlesticks! You obviously haven't heard what the village gossips have to say about me. Or have you? And is that why you don't want to risk being seen alone with me?'

Roy shook his head. 'If you put it like that, you leave me no choice. When shall I call for you? If there's no cloud cover, that is'

Faith giggled. 'Come... Come to tea; and never mind about the cloud.'

Mary seemed pleased that her son had been invited out to tea again. 'And on the eve of your birthday, too,' she said.

Roy frowned. 'But with Faith and Charity? Is that wise?'

'Wise? Why shouldn't it be?'

'Well... What I mean is - hasn't Faith a bit of a reputation?'

'She certainly has; not only is she a first-rate teacher, she's a fine organist and choir mistress as well.'

'Mother, you know that's not what I mean. Don't play games.'

Mary gave vent to an enigmatic little laugh. 'Oh I see! You mean **that** kind of reputation. Well, you needn't concern yourself with that. Faith's not bothered about having that kind of reputation.'

Roy was aghast. 'You mean… You mean, it's true what they say about her?'

Mary nodded. 'Yes - well, I suspect much of it is.'

'And you still don't mind my going to see her?'

'No, why should I? I've known Faith all her life and I can tell you, you're better with her than with some loose-minded young girl. And goodness knows, there's plenty of those around these parts.'

'Mother, you surprise me!'

Again Mary laughed. 'Life's full of surprises! But you can take it from me, Faith's not one of them. With her, it's always been a case of, what you see is what you get. She tells me that, when this weather's over, she intends to buy herself a car, and you'll need someone to take you to the Morris dancing classes. And she may even offer to teach you to drive. That's more than you can expect from some young mawther.'[1*]

Roy sighed. 'Oh very well then! On your own head be it!'

Looking straight at him, Mary giggled. It was infectious, and having joined in, he went to fetch his skates. He was

---

[1*] Mawther = a girl

lucky to have any. They'd been lent him by Lord Denver, who had sent word to ask if any of his staff would like the loan of skates as there were several old pairs stored away at the hall. Roy had been one of the first to apply and, having found a pair to fit him, he had lost no time in putting his skating skills to the test. With his considerable dancing skills proving their worth when it came to learning to maintain his balance, he was soon skating around with the best of them on the thickly frozen lake in the park.

Tea at Kiln House was a pleasant affair. Charity was no less pleased to see Roy than was Faith, even though she was dubious about skating in the moonlight. But Faith was in no mood to listen. 'We'll wrap up against the cold and the exercise will do us good,' she said.

Faith always used an old pair of skating boots that had belonged to her mother, who had been born in 1865. Winters had been more severe when she was young and she and her future husband had often skated together in their young days. It was as she was searching the cupboard under the stairs for an old pair of her father's skates that she thought Roy might find more suitable than the ones he had borrowed from the hall that Charity called to her from the front door to say that a cloud had just covered the rising moon. Roy followed Faith to the door to look out. 'It's a bank of cloud blowing up on a strengthening east wind,' he said.

Half an hour later it was snowing heavily. There would be no skating that night. Roy was for setting out for home right away, but Charity advised against it. 'It's turning into a blizzard,' she said. 'I'll telephone Mary to tell her we're keeping you here for the night. Then we'll get a couple of hot jars[2*] into the big bed to make sure it's well aired.'

Later, as they were all seated together in the living room, Faith remarked that it was a shame Roy hadn't brought his violin with him, but Charity disagreed. 'If he was playing, he couldn't dance, and he's such a good dancer,' she said.

Taking the hint, Faith moved across to the piano. Soberly clad in trousers and a warm green jumper, she seemed unusually subdued, a condition that wasn't, however, reflected in her playing, which commenced with the stirring rhythms of a brisk polka.

'Hold on!' Charity exclaimed. 'Give us a chance to move the furniture.'

This time the dancing was even more enjoyable than it had been on Boxing Day, and time passed quickly. As they rested between dances, Roy remarked that it didn't seem fair that Faith never got a chance to dance, but Charity wasn't bothered. 'Oh, she doesn't mind!' she said with some nonchalance. 'She's not much of a dancer anyway. She's always preferred playing to dancing - and singing, of course. That's an idea! Sing to us Faith.'

Accompanying herself on the piano, Faith obliged with a rendering of 'Down by the Sally Gardens'. Roy was impressed by the richness of her mezzo-soprano voice. After the song was finished, she turned round, telling Roy that he ought to attend church. 'You'd enjoy the music,' she said.

'But I'm not religious,' Roy protested. 'Besides, I don't much like the rector.'

2* Hot jars = Stone heating jars, the forerunners of hot water bottles, were still being used at that time.

Faith adopted a doleful tone. 'Poor Reverend Thurlow! He's not **that** bad, surely?'

Charity changed the subject, saying she would see if she could find some pyjamas for Roy to sleep in. After she had gone, Roy helped Faith move the furniture back in place. After the job was done, she bade him follow her upstairs to find out where he was to sleep. Kiln House had four bedrooms and Faith and Charity still slept in the same rooms they had used from their childhoods. As for Roy, they had decided to put him in their late parents' bedroom, where the double bed was already made up in expectation of a visit from a cousin of theirs and her husband, weather permitting. Since the war had delayed the arrival of electricity in the village, Faith lit a candle to light their way upstairs. Once in the large bedroom, she lit the lamp that stood on a table near the bedside. 'You'll like it in here,' she said.

As they stood talking, Charity brought the pyjamas and laid them on the bed, asking if he would be needing anything else. Roy shook his head. 'No, I don't think so, and if you don't mind, I think I'll turn in for the night.'

'A good idea, and I think I'll do the same. I must confess that dancing with you has quite tired me out,' Charity said before adding with a short laugh: 'So, I'll bid you goodnight and leave you in Faith's tender care.'

After she had gone, Faith said: 'I'll leave you to get undressed.'

Having undressed, neatly folded his clothes and placed them on a nearby chair, Roy donned the pyjamas and got into bed, where he was grateful for the warmth from the two stone jars. He was just wondering what to do about putting out the light, when the door opened and Faith re-entered the room. Roy gasped. The jumper and trousers had been replaced by a richly embroidered, red negligee.

'We thought it best that you should not be left to sleep alone in a strange house,' she said in a matter of fact tone of voice as she closed the door behind her, before stepping into the lamp light and removing the negligee with a saucy flourish. Realising that any attempt at trying to escape from the trap he was caught in would be a complicated business, Roy swallowed hard and awaited developments as Faith posed for his pleasure clad in nothing more than bra, suspender belt, stockings and close fitting red knickers. Bending forward and reaching behind her, she unfastened her bra and slipped out of it. Roy gasped. He was thrilling to the view of a whole new landscape unfolding before him. It was as if the winter ice had melted to reveal a rolling landscape bursting into bloom with spring flowers. Casting her bra aside and with her breasts bouncing, Faith twirled round, pushing her ample backside towards him, as she began to wriggle out of her scant knickers with exaggerated endeavour until they fell down her legs revealing the full fascination of her buttocks bouncing above the power of her pleasure-filled thighs. Roy was reminded of a plough horse in trace harness as he drank deeply of her desirability, hoping the while that she wouldn't strip further.

Wise enough not to, Faith pulled the bed clothes back and climbed onto the bed. Straddling his form under the bedclothes, she cupped her right breast in her hand, bringing the tempting rosiness of its firm nipple up close to his face. In a kind of instinctive way, Roy knew he must suck it; but as he made to do so, Faith moved aside saying she must remove the stone heating jars. Having done so, she then lay beside him so as to bring her shapely breasts in line with his mouth. Turning towards her, Roy reached out to fondle her thighs and buttocks as he nosed into her breasts, searching for a nipple with his mouth. Allowing him to suck away at it for a while, Faith asked him in a dreamy tone of voice if this was the first time he had done such a thing. When he said it was, she professed disbelief.

'But it's the truth!' he protested.

'Not according to what I hear. I have it on very good authority that you used to delight in sucking another woman's breasts for the best part of a year.'

'What nonsense! Whoever told you that?'

'Someone I know called Mary.'

'I don't know a girl called Mary.'

'What about your mother?'

'My mother? Oh, I see! You mean when I was a baby?'

Faith chuckled. 'What else should I mean? Anyway, don't stop sucking mine; I'm enjoying it far too much for you to stop now.'

After some time, Roy changed to the other breast as Faith began to fondle his erection. Presently, she began talking to him again, telling him that his current experience was in the way of being a seventeenth birthday present from the Sisterhood. Roy didn't understand, but Faith was reluctant to explain further, saying that, one day, he would discover its meaning. 'It's something that can't be told, only discovered,' she said before adding in an urgent tone of voice: 'But enough of that. You must hold me close now and kiss me on the mouth.'

Just as Roy was wishing that the kiss would never end, Faith broke free and began to turn him gently over onto his back, at the same contriving to kneel upright astride him so as to allow his erect penis to slide up inside her. Looking up at her bathed in light from the nearby lamp, Roy thought how enticingly desirable she was from the fullness of her sensuous lips down through the bouncing of her ample breasts to the firm rotundity of her abdomen above the line of the suspender belt that she still had on, its long suspenders running down her thighs seeming to emphasise their power as she began to wriggle and move up and down. It was as if he were journeying through the undulations of a freshly clad, spring landscape resplendent in the first flush of blackthorn blossom and sweet scent of primroses. Stimulated thus by both sight and motion, it wasn't long before Roy experienced a vast thrill, the joy of which he could never have imagined possible. Then, as his ecstasy subsided into a warm glow of satisfaction as his erection slackened, Faith rolled over onto her side and took his right hand into hers saying she would now show him how to give her satisfaction. Rejoicing in the velvet softness of her, Roy stimulated away for a while until her joyful cry signified that she had achieved orgasm. Soon afterwards, having removed the suspender belt and stockings, she snuggled up to him for more hugging and fondling. An hour or so later, coupling with her for a second ride, this time in more conventional fashion, he knew what to do to bring her to orgasm along with himself before he dismounted. Then, in the immediate aftermath, he wished he could sleep with her forever.

The following morning, Faith was up before he awoke.

Bringing him a cup of tea, she sat on the bed and asked if he would like to go to church with her and Charity.

Roy shook his head. 'Stay here with me and let Charity go on her own.'

'You know I can't do that; I have to play the organ.'

'Why yes, of course, you're a first rate organ player.'

Faith giggled. 'When it comes to that, you're not so bad yourself. Many men have lived all their lives and not achieved what you achieved for me last night.'

Reality dawning, Roy frowned. 'Heavens! What if I've made you pregnant!'

Faith shook her head. 'Have no fear, no one has ever been able to do that. That's how it is with some women.'

Roy's relief turned to concern. 'But would you not want to have a child?'

Faith shook her head. 'No, it's not for me. I'd rather teach. It gives you more children than any womb possibly could, and I don't think I could cope with children at home as well as at school. Now, with Charity, it's different. I feel she should have married and had children.'

'And she can have children?.'

Faith nodded. 'Yes, indeed. That's why you've had me and not her.'

'You mean, she would've liked to…'

Again Faith nodded. 'Sleep with you? Yes, and she would have but for the risk, and she doesn't like condoms and that kind of thing.'

Roy had heard of those. He wanted to know more. Being with Faith was like being thrown in at the deep end. Fortunately for him, she was a good teacher and he had learned to 'swim' quickly. Having explained everything as best she could, Faith was suddenly serious. 'Tell me, Roy, what do you truly think of me. I mean, for one thing, do you…?'

'Do I love you? Yes I do and always will, but it's not the same as what they call "falling in love". Love like that is having a crush on someone and I don't have one of those on you. No, it's more like as if you were - well, what you are - a teacher - my teacher, my very special loving, caring teacher and one I can love and respect in return. Maybe I'm a bit young to be doing what we did and many would say we did wrong, but I don't care. I don't feel as if there's anything wrong about it. I think it's often the **way** things are done that makes them right or wrong.'

Faith's eyes twinkled. 'And you don't think your mother will mind?'

'Mind? But she needn't…' Stopping suddenly, Roy leaned forward and looked straight into Faith's eyes. 'But that's just it! She does know, doesn't she? You and her - the two of you - you planned it between you!'

Nodding slowly, Faith giggled. 'We did indeed and we should have known better than to have tried to deceive you. You're too much of your mother's son for anyone to be able to do that for long.'

Roy was embarrassed. He didn't like the thought of his mother knowing what he and Faith had done together.

Sensing his discomfiture, Faith sought to reassure him.

'Mary sees a good future for you in the gardening world. She doesn't want you side-tracked at too early an age by any love interest that might lead you into undesirable company. I can do things for you that she can't and she knows you're safe with me, that I'll mother you in way she isn't able to do. After all, I'm little more than three years younger than she is. So there's no need to be embarrassed. Just remember: the Sisterhood understands.'

Roy drank some tea. Then, setting the cup back in its saucer, he said in a wistful tone of voice: 'Ah yes! The Sisterhood! You mentioned it last night, and it's something special isn't it? I mean, it's more than just a name for a collection of women who happen to be friendly with each other.'

Faith nodded. 'That's right, but I'm afraid you'll have to find out more about it of your own volition. You're not going to find any woman living any where round here who's going to tell you anything about it. However, I can give you just one clue. You've heard of Haddingham's Hollow?'

Roy nodded. 'You mean about a couple of miles west of the Ashden Estate in Felsham parish where yeoman farmer Bob Rookyard farms?'

'That's right.' An enigmatic smile flickered around a corner of Faith's sensuous lips as she continued: 'It's where a brook, a tributary of the River Deben, runs through a long, narrow copse out through some water meadows. On some high ground to the north of them, there's an old ruin hidden inside a spinney. Have you been there?'

Roy shook his head. 'No; but I've seen it from a distance and know where you mean. My dad says it's called Lisa's Lodge after a witch or wisewoman who once used to live there. They say it's the farthest point round here from any metalled road. I was always told never to go there as the Rookyards didn't like people walking on their land. But I don't understand. How can it be a clue?'

Faith stood up. 'Well now, that's for you to find out. Anyway, enjoy your tea and then get dressed and come down to breakfast.'

Roy beckoned for her to stay. 'Just a moment! I want... I mean, I want to tell you something. Your whole body - all of you... It's... Well, it's like a beautiful landscape - a heavenly place where it's a joy to be alive.'

Bending over him, Faith kissed him on the forehead. 'You're a dear, dear boy, and I want you know that I'm here for you - always.' And with that she was away and gone from the room.

Not many people made it to church that morning. Yet again the roads were blocked with drifts, as Roy discovered as he made his way home, where his parents and brother chorused him a happy birthday. Later, when he was alone with his mother in the kitchen, he made a point of thanking her for his birthday presents.

Mary shrugged. 'Oh that's all right. You don't need to thank me a second time. It's just that we thought that a new shirt and a couple of pairs of socks would always come in handy.'

'Don't be obtuse, mother. I don't mean what you, dad and Fred together have given me. I mean... Well, Faith and all that.'

'Faith and all that? What's that supposed to mean?'

'I think you know what it means.'

Turning to face Roy, Mary looked him straight in the face. 'What I know is my business; what Faith knows is her business; and the kind of relationship the two of you have together is your business. All I will say is that I've known Faith all her life and I trust her. You say often enough that you never want to leave the village. The best way to achieve that is for you to work your way up to becoming head gardener at the Hall. So I suggest you concentrate on doing just that and leave Faith and me to work away at the things the two of us know best about.'

Impressed by Mary's emphatic attitude, Roy refrained from pressing the matter. Going outside, he lent a hand at clearing the snow from the paths. Later on, after tea, he practised away at his violin before retiring for the night. He was glad to be alone. As wonderful as she was, he wouldn't want to sleep with Faith too often - sometimes, certainly, but on special occasions. His final thoughts before falling asleep were concerning Lisa's Lodge. What had Faith been trying to tell him?

Chapter 3

Knickers

It was over five years later and Mary had called to see Faith at Kiln Cottage in the afternoon of a bright June day during her school's mid term Whitsun break. The two of them were becoming increasingly concerned about Roy's love life, which didn't seem to have progressed very much, if at all, since his first erotic encounter with Faith. If it hadn't been for her husband, Roy's father William, she mightn't have been so bothered, but being twenty years older than her, he was wanting to retire into the cottage where his oldest son Fred now lived with his wife and two small children so that Fred could bring his family to live at the wheelwright's residence, where he had already taken over the running of the business. With Roy now in his twenty third year, Mary had hoped that he might at least have a steady girl friend, something that would go some way to convincing Hunter, Lord Denver's agent, that he intended to marry and was thus worth considering as a tenant for a vacant cottage on the estate.

'It would be so much nicer if he could move into his own cottage at the same time as we exchange dwellings with Fred,' Mary said, looking across the kitchen table at Faith, who was seated opposite her at its far end. Realising that her presence would not be welcome, Charity had gone out into the garden to get on with some weeding. Faith thought it might be a good idea if someone could have a word with Lord Denver, but Mary shook her head. 'What good would that do? He's so unapproachable; always insists on doing all that kind of thing through that awful Hunter.'

'Well, that's true enough,' Faith agreed. 'But I think there's a way to get round that - if you leave it to me, that is.'

'You mean, you know something I don't?'

Faith nodded. 'Hmm… You could say that.'.

Knowing Faith well enough to realise that it was pointless to press her further on the matter, Mary turned to discussing Roy's prospects, which were now very good. With one of the two assistant gardeners having retired and the other having moved on to take up a head gardener's job, he was now number two to John Lankester, the head gardener, who was due to retire within less than six years. With Lord Denver very impressed with Roy's abilities, there was every chance of his succeeding John in the top job, a prestigious post in one of the top gardens in the county, besides which Lord Denver was planning to open it to the public on selected days. Agreeing that it was virtually certain that Roy would eventually become head gardener, Faith said she thought they must try harder to find him a suitable partner.

A worried look on her face, Mary looked straight at Faith. 'I wonder… Look, please don't be offended if I say this, but you don't think, well, that he's sort of, well, fallen in love with you - or you with him for that matter? And that's why…'

Faith shook her head, quite vigorously. 'No, there's none of that, and here's why: he never acts like a besotted lover. As for myself, you know me well enough to know that falling in love is not part of my psyche. Give me so called "lust" every time; it's more honest.'

Mary looked relieved. 'Well that's all right then. And as for Roy, you think he, too, might be like that - lustful, I mean?'

Faith laughed. 'Well... Well, in a way, yes, and then, no. He's actually very fond of me and I of him, but it's the love of friendship. It's like two friends helping each other out. You know what a libido I have. Realising that, he enjoys trying to satisfy me - that kind of thing. Then again, I suppose there's an element of protectionism in it - protecting him from falling for the wrong kind of girl. Only, well, I'm concerned lest it gets out of hand and lasts too long. I teach him to drive; he passes the test; he uses my car; doesn't bother to see about buying one of his own and so on. That kind of thing, if you see what I mean.'

Mary did. 'It's all such a comfortable, convenient rut,' she said.

Faith smiled knowingly. 'Like I say, leave it to me. There's a way of handling Lord Denver and getting the better of Hunter at the same time.'

The two women went on to discuss Lisa's Lodge. Since Faith had first brought it to Roy's attention over five years ago, he had never been there. Since he knew all the footpaths for miles around and was a great explorer of the countryside, Faith thought this was very surprising; but Mary wasn't so sure. 'It's the Rookyards,' she said. 'Roy knows they don't like people on their land, even on the footpaths, and he's not the kind to seek unnecessary confrontation.'

Faith could understand that. 'Then, of course, there's his music and Morris dancing, which take up much of his spare time. Anyway, it's all to the good. We don't really want him going there too soon, do we? At least not until…'

As Faith, a saucy twinkle in her eyes, stopped in mid sentence, Mary giggled in a distinctly girl-like fashion that belied her years. 'We… We certainly don't. That's why you need to put the pressure on Lord Denver as soon as you can.' As proud of her son as she was, she would not be entirely satisfied until he had fulfilled his true destiny - whatever that might be.

Several footpaths intersected the deer park on the Ashden Estate and people were allowed to walk round the outside of the deer-proof fence that surrounded the lake with its three wooded islands. Since the deer had plenty of ponds at their disposal throughout the park it had long been thought best not to risk them disturbing the lake, which was a haven for all kinds of water fowl and other wildlife. As Faith sat down on one of the several seats dotted around the lake inside the protective fence, she was unfazed by the fact that only members of Lord Denver's family and his close friends were allowed in there. Since she and the old man went back a long way, she knew that he wasn't going to take exception to her being there during his early morning walk. That's if he was taking it that morning. Since it was a long standing habit of his to do so almost every fine day during the summer months, she had high hopes of meeting him on that bright June morning. Sure enough, she hadn't to wait long before he came walking briskly into view.

'Faith! What a pleasant surprise! I didn't expect to see you here.'

Faith patted the seat beside her. 'Come and sit down you old lecher.'

Doing as he was bid, Lord Denver protested at being so called, but Faith just laughed. 'There's something you want of me, otherwise you wouldn't be here,' he said.

Shifting up close to him, Faith placed an arm around his shoulders. 'Do as I ask and I'll give you a good time in the boat house for old time's sake.'

'For old time's sake, eh? Well, as it turns out, I could do with some cheering up this morning. So you'd best get on with telling me what else you want of me.'

Although both Faith and Lord Denver were late for their breakfasts that morning, since both had got what they wanted, neither of them minded in the least. He had been pleasured in a thrilling fashion that he knew only Faith was capable of and she had ensured that he would tell Hunter to give the cottage to Roy. Delighted by the news, Charity wanted to know how she had managed to persuade the old boy.

Removing her knickers from her dress pocket, Faith threw them in among the dirty washing. 'How do you think? But it was hard for the old boy. In the end I had to masturbate him. But he did the same for me and it was worth it all,' she explained nonchalantly before sitting down, knickerless, to breakfast.

Charity laughed. 'What **are** we going to do with you? You're lucky you've got me to watch over you. I dread to think what Parson Thurlow would do if he found out that his organist was little better than an obliging tart.'

Faith giggled. 'Going by his battleaxe of a wife, he'd be round here asking for favours, I shouldn't wonder, and who would blame him?'

'You're incorrigible!' Charity exclaimed before indulging in another peel of laughter. Despite her deep religious convictions - or perhaps because of them - she could never bring herself to condemn her sister for her seemingly loose morals.

At around ten o'clock that same morning Parson Thurlow called in at Kiln House to discuss the music for the church services, his reasoning being that the Whitsun break afforded them the extra time to get the music sorted out for the services for the ensuing six Sundays or more. This would also have the added advantage of allowing Faith to get on with the choir practices without having to consult with him before each one. This being so, Faith was pleased to see him, and they spent sometime together with the piano in the sitting room. What he would have done if he had known she was knickerless during the whole period of his stay, Faith didn't dare to think. The main thing was, she enjoyed training the choir and he was more than grateful for having such a skilled and dedicated organist. And anyway, she liked the neat little man with his greying dark hair, brown eyes and neat, pointy nose. Well into his fifties as he was, she couldn't help wondering what had persuaded him to marry such a large woman taller than himself. What was their sex life like? Indeed, had there been any sex at all between them since the birth of their only child, a daughter who was now a dentist and practised in Ipswich, where she had bought a house and lived alone? Since he had been their rector for little more than three years, Faith and

Charity didn't know that much about his background, but they were beginning to like him a lot. His devoted pastoral care, devoid of evangelical fervour, appealed to their sense of proportion. Evangelicalism might do very well in suburbia, but it didn't go down well with village bred Anglicans, whose attitude was that, if folk wanted that kind of thing they should go to the chapel, which in that part of Suffolk always meant Baptist.

As Parson Thurlow was about to leave, Charity came into the hall to say goodbye. He apologised for neglecting her. 'Faith gets all my attention. You can blame the music,' he said.

Charity beamed him a bright smile. 'Then I certainly will. After all, it's like the old song: *It's the girl who plays the organ gets her man.*'

Parson Thurlow looked puzzled. 'I'm afraid I don't know that one, but it certainly fit's the bill this time.' He turned to go as Faith held the front door open for him only to pause on the threshold and turn to look straight at Charity again us he exclaimed in no uncertain terms: 'Knickers!' Then, seeing Charity's eyes widen in surprise, he explained: 'I mean… Well, you see, it's Flora, my wife. I always like to buy her something a little special for her birthday. You know, something unexpected that I know she'll like, and she does like frilly, pretty things. So this year I thought of underwear - frilly knickers, that kind of thing - but I want it to be a surprise and, you see, it's a bit difficult…'

Charity came to the rescue. 'And you'd like one of us to get them for you? Any idea of her size?'

'Well, her hip measurement is 38.'

'Fine; then I'll get you several pairs. You can pay me later. Now, have you any idea of design, colour - that sort of thing?'

'Well, it's hard to be precise…'

'Yes, of course, I understand. Look, I have a ladies underwear catalogue. If you can spare a little more of your time, perhaps we could go through it together. Or better still, Faith will look at it with you in the sitting room. I need to get on with preparing lunch.'

Faith was very helpful and she soon had half a dozen suitable designs sorted out for the good man. He was most grateful. 'Her birthday's on the first of July,' he said. 'Perhaps you would be kind enough to keep them here until the day before?'

'I'll certainly do that, **and** wrap them up for you, if you like.'

'You're most kind. Please feel free to buy a pair for yourself. I mean, if you wear them - I mean these fancy designs.'

'Well, I certainly do sometimes. Thank you!'

After the good man had finally gone, Faith joined her sister in the kitchen, where the two of them erupted into fits of laughter until the tears ran down their cheeks.

Chapter 4

Verity

It was almost two years later and Roy still hadn't found a girl friend. When Mary chided him about it, his standard response was always that, what with his job, his music and his Morris dancing he just didn't have the time to go out with girls. Tactfully refraining from pointing out that he could still find time for Faith and Charity, Mary took comfort in the fact that he had recently bought a car, thus reducing his dependency on Faith. But Roy didn't see it that way. As far as he was concerned he wasn't dependent on anyone, not even on Lord Denver for giving him a job. With head gardener, John Lankester, not in the best of health and due to retire soon, he was becoming as near to indispensable as anyone could expect to get. As for his private life, he had become adept at looking after himself. Having moved into Rose Cottage with its large garden at the end of a short, tarmacked cul-de-sac known as Bumber Lane, he had lost no time in learning how to prepare his own food. In this respect he had been greatly helped by his mother and Charity, both of whom had been diligent in teaching him the essentials. He was also helped by the fact that the village had been connected to mains water, sewerage and electricity since 1952.

There were four other dwellings in Bumber lane, two

on either side. Roy's parents had moved into the first one on the left facing towards Rose Cottage, which was convenient for Roy to drop in for some of his meals, and he was always welcome to eat with Faith and Charity. Ashden was an isolated village with no main road to anywhere running through it. Bumber Lane opened onto the main village road directly opposite Saint Mary's Parish Church on the far side of Ashden Common, now more in the nature of being the village green. The main entrance leading to Ashden Hall was situated down a side road that branched off on the far side of the church. A few shops of one kind and another surrounded the green. The only traditional village item lacking was a public house or inn of any kind. For some reason, the village inn, known as The Green Man, was situated almost a mile in a southerly direction along the main road leading out of the village. Although there must have been a reason for such a citing, not even the oldest village inhabitant knew what it was.

Roy soon found that the main problem with living alone was keeping the cottage clean. Mary suggested that he asked Verity Page if she would go in one morning a week and clean for him. Since her little girl, Jane, had recently started school Verity was looking for part time work. Best of all, she lived in Mousehole Cottage, the dwelling in Bumber Lane nearest to Rose Cottage. She was married to Dan Page, the head park keeper, one of whose jobs was to cull the deer and butcher the carcases. Verity had been just twenty when she married Dan, who was fifteen years her senior. Notwithstanding the age difference, they were noted in the village for being a contented and well balanced couple, although there were some who wondered that Verity had not had at least another child - to keep Jane company, as they say.

After lunch the following Saturday, on a bracing March day not long after his twenty fifth birthday, Roy popped across to Mousehole Cottage to ask if Verity would clean for him. Not being able to get an answer to his knock on the front door, he went round to the back, where he found her pushing Jane on a swing Dan had rigged up for her on the sturdy branch of an oak tree growing in the thick hedge at the foot of the long back garden. Somewhat reluctantly, Jane agreed to go inside and play with her teddy bears.

'She likes dressing them up,' Verity explained. 'Doesn't like dolls.' Leading the way indoors, she indicated a chair by the kitchen table. Then, seating herself in another one at its opposite end, she said in an inquisitorial tone of voice: 'So then, how long is it we've been neighbours?'

Taken aback by such unexpected directness, Roy faltered: 'How long? Well… it's close on two years.'

'Two years? And this is the first time you've been to see me?'

'Well yes; but then, you've never been to see me.'

'Maybe not, but Dan has.'

'So he has, but that's because we both work for the same boss.'

'Work, work, work! It's all work with you, isn't it?'

'I'm certainly kept busy. But talking of work, I've come to ask if you'd do some work for me - housework, that is.'

'It depends on for how long and when. I'm free all day on Fridays.'

So it was agreed that Verity would clean for Roy for three hours on Friday mornings. He would provide her with a spare key to enable access whilst he was at work. Although he agreed to pay her the going rate, if she made a good job of the cleaning, he had it in mind to pay her a little more on account of his just having received an increase in wages to compensate him for his extra responsibilities now that he was preparing to take over from John Lankester. He was just about to rise to take his leave when Verity asked if he would like to stay for a while over a pot of tea. Somewhat reluctantly, as he had work he wanted to be getting on with in the garden at Rose Cottage, he agreed. Then, as Verity stood up to make the tea, he asked after Dan.

'He's gone to Ipswich - to the football match,' she said, reaching for the tea caddy. 'Goes every other week, he does. Catches the Eastern Counties bus with his mates at the stop at Buxley Cross the other side of the Green Man. Dan likes his football.' She reached for the kettle boiling on the stove and began to wet the tea. 'Fact is, I don't see much of him again till passed eleven o'clock of a Saturday evening. On their return from the match, they always stop off at the Green Man, where they enjoy a drink together and play darts. Is it one sugar or two?'

'Just the one please,' Watching her as she moved around, Roy was wondering how any man would ever want leave such a fine looking woman to go drinking with his mates. Then, as he sipped his tea, he complimented her on how well she had made it. 'It's just as I like it - wet and weak. So many people always spoil tea by making it too strong, I always think.'

Verity flashed him a bright smile. 'Funny you should say that. I'm afraid I was being selfish - that is, making the tea to suit myself. Now, Dan, he always likes real strong, spoon supporting stuff. It makes a real change sharing tea with a man - another person - who has the same tastes as myself - at least in one way, I mean.'

As he took a longer pull at his tea, Roy feasted his eyes on her over the rim of the cup. Strange that he had never really noticed her before. She was really a very attractive women. Replacing the cup in its saucer he remarked that she wasn't a village girl.

Verity shook her head. 'No, I'm not; but not far away, all the same. I was born and brought up in Felsham and I went to school at Teddlethwaite. As a matter of fact, I was taught by Faith Littlemore. She's a friend of yours, isn't she?'

Roy nodded. 'She and her sister Charity both are - my friends, I mean.'

Verity looked away. 'Sometimes one needs good friends,' she said wistfully.

As he sat there looking at her, a neat, slender girl clad in a red, high-necked jumper and black slacks, her shoulder-length, fair hair framing her neatly chiselled features dominated by the honest brightness of her inviting blue eyes. Suddenly he said: 'I'm.. Well, it's Saturday afternoons. I mean, you're always welcome… And Jane too, of course. Tea… I mean…'

Looking straight at him, Verity laughed. 'That's an invitation to tea, I take it. Well, I don't always know about the tea, but I will come to see you on Saturdays, if only to get paid. That I promise.' She giggled before continuing. 'But what about Faith? Wouldn't you rather be going to see her?'

Roy blushed. 'Why should I want to do that?'

'You tell me! From what I understand, the two of you have a lot going for each other.'

Roy stood up. 'Well, yes, maybe. Now, if you'll excuse me, I'd better be going. Thanks for the tea. And… Well, I'll drop a spare key into you later.'

Following him outside, she said suddenly. 'I'll come back with you and get it now - I mean, the key.' Then, stepping back inside, she called for Jane to come with her.

Jane was delighted with Roy's garden. She ran around exploring every nook and cranny. Verity admonished her, but Roy told her to leave her be. 'Come inside whilst I find the spare key,' he added as he opened the back door. 'There, sit yourself down. Let me see now, where did I put it…'

'Your kitchen's bigger than ours,' Jane remarked enthusiastically as she ran inside.

Roy opened a door that led into the front hall. 'There, go and explore,' he said. 'You can go upstairs. Count all the rooms and tell me how many there are.' He watched the little girl as she ran upstairs. Then, as he came back into the kitchen, Verity greeted him with a surprised look.

'You like children?' she said.

Roy sat down at the far end of the table, which had a pine top and was longer than the one in Verity's kitchen. 'I don't know,' he said. 'But Jane seems such a happy little girl.'

Agreeing, Verity added wistfully: 'But she gets a bit lonely at times. There's no one of her age group at this end of the village and - well, she's no brothers and sisters either.'

'You hope for more? I mean, children?'

Lowering her gaze, Verity nodded. 'Yes, I would. Not too many, of course. In fact one more would be just fine.'

'And you… I mean, you still…?'

'Oh yes, we still try. That's to say, now and then.'

'I see… Well, you never know…' Roy was struggling for suitable words.

Lifting her head, Verity turned to look at him along the length of the table as she gave vent to a hollow laugh. 'Never is a long time,' she said.

Remembering that the spare key was hanging with some other keys in the cupboard under the stairs, he stood up to go and get it just as Jane burst into the room informing him that the house had ten rooms: 'Three bedrooms, one landing, three downstairs rooms, one hall and a bathroom and toilet,' she said.

Roy laughed. 'Ah! But the landing isn't a room,' he said.

Jane disagreed. 'Well, it has it's own space; so I think it is.'

'Its own space? Very well then, ten it is.' Roy went to fetch the key.

Minutes later, he followed Verity outside as she was leaving, holding Jane firmly by the hand. Suddenly, Roy didn't want her to go. 'Verity! I mean, you don't mind my calling you that?' he called after her.

'No; why should I? We're neighbours, aren't we?' she retorted as she turned back to face him.

'Yes. Yes, of course; but what I mean is - well, you will come to see me again, won't you? I mean, not just on Fridays when I'm not here; but… Well, like today…'

'Like today…' Verity echoed before adding as she turned away again: 'Yes, of course. Otherwise, how am I going to get paid?'

Standing at his front gate, Roy watched the two of them until they had disappeared from view round the back of their own cottage. Then, with a sigh, he returned to his back garden to get on with some work. Used to working on his own, loneliness had never been a problem for him. That is, not until now when, suddenly, a surge of emptiness, bringing on a feeling of intense isolation, overwhelmed him, causing him to leave off planting potatoes to go and sit down on an old garden bench. Leaning forward, he held his head in his hands.

Teatime at Kiln House the following day was an unusually taciturn occasion with both Charity and Faith sensing that something had occurred to distress the usually affable Roy, who always had tea with them on Sundays whenever possible. Saying that she would wash up on her own for once, Charity insisted that Faith go and keep Roy company in the sitting room, where she lost no time asking him if anything had occurred to distress him. He shook his head, but Faith was not deceived. 'I think you had better tell me,' she said.

'I don't know what to say,' Roy protested.

Suddenly Faith knew. 'It's a woman, isn't it?' she said, looking straight at him.

Roy nodded. He looked at the floor. 'I think you might well be right.'

'You mean, you've met someone you like? Then, why so glum?'

Roy threw her a despairing glance. 'It's not as simple as that.'

'So? Nothing is ever simple. Problems are there to be solved.'

'Then, solve this one. She's a married women.'

'And you've fallen in love with her?'

Roy nodded. Rising to his feet he went and knelt beside Faith's chair and hugged her. 'Oh Faith, why couldn't I have fallen in love with you?'

Returning his embrace, Faith murmured; 'Because it would have spoiled things between us. I've mothered you as the son I never had and we've given each other deep and meaningful sexual satisfaction. It's my belief that you can't have that kind of love and affection and fall in love at the same time. It's like trying to play rugger on a football pitch. Now, would you like to tell me who it is?'

The following Saturday afternoon, when Verity came to collect her money, Jane wasn't with her. Inviting her in, Roy asked after the child.

Verity went and sat down at the end of the kitchen table. 'She's with Dan - in the garden. Ipswich are playing away this week. He'll not be here next Saturday afternoon when they'll be playing at home. He'll be off to the Green Man after tea. So, I thought I'd come and see you before there's Jane for me to see to.'

Not knowing what else to do, Roy sat down at the other end of the table. 'You can always bring her with you,' he said.

Turning her head to glance anxiously along the length of the table to where Roy was profiled against the light of the westering sun beaming in through the window at the far end of the kitchen, Verity said quickly: 'You like her, don't you?'

Turning his head, Roy looked straight into her blue eyes. 'Yes, I do. She's so vibrant.' He looked away before adding. 'But then, of course, I know nothing about children.'

'Nothing about children…' Verity echoed slowly before adding briskly: 'I didn't tell her I was coming here. I'll… I'll bring her to see you next Saturday. If that's all right, I mean…'

'Oh yes, it's all right. But it's nice to see you too, of course. I mean, to have you to do the cleaning. You made a good job of it.'

Verity looked at the floor. 'I do my best.'

Roy opened his mouth to say something; then, lost for words, closed it again. Fearing Verity would leave as soon as he paid her, he was reluctant to give her the money too soon. As it was, she seemed in no hurry to leave, and the two of them sat together in silence for what seemed a long time, before she suddenly said: 'Next Saturday: if you like… if you like, when I bring Jane - we could come to tea.'

Turning round in his chair to look straight along the table at her, Roy echoed: 'Could come to tea? You're inviting me to tea?'

'No, silly! You're inviting me!'

'Am I? Well, if you say so…'

Standing up, Verity walked around the table to stand beside him. Placing an arm across his shoulders she patted him gently on the back as she said softly: 'If it's all right with you, I'll take the money now.'

Reaching behind him, Roy held her hand for a few seconds before rising to his feet and feeling for his wallet in the back pocket of his trousers. Since Verity had barely moved, she was standing very close to him, making it difficult for him to get the money into her hand. Much taller than her, he found himself looking down at the top of her head as he placed the correct amount in a tiny hand that seemed to have been fashioned for anything but hard work. Stepping away, she suddenly asked if he was going to Kiln House for tea the following day.

'Yes. Yes, I am; but you needn't mind…'

'Mind? Why should I mind?'

'I don't know… I just thought… Well, I mean…'

Verity suddenly burst out laughing. 'Mean… Mean? Why should I care what you mean?' She moved towards the back door. Seconds later, she was gone.

'Wake up! Wake up!' Something was pushing at Roy's shoulder. Drowsy from having only recently fallen into the first thralls of sleep, he struggled to sit up in bed as the voice continued: 'Come! I need your help.'

It was Verity. Having let herself in with her key, she had come to ask Roy to help her find Dan, who had failed to return from the Green Man. He was usually home no later than half eleven, but it was now well passed midnight. She waited in the kitchen while Roy got dressed. Minutes later, picking up a torch, he followed her outside, where she begged him to go and see if he could find Dan. 'I'd go myself, only I can't leave Jane alone for that long,' she said.

Deciding to take the car, Roy was soon driving slowly along the road that led to the Green Man, but there was no sign of anyone in the glare of the headlights, and not a single light was to be seen in the Green Man. Thinking at first that he would knock them up and ask after Dan, he then thought better of it in favour of driving back along the road to enable him to scrutinise the other side of the road with greater accuracy. He was almost back to the junction with the road round the common when he noticed the wheel protruding from a ditch. Stopping the car, he got out with his torch to have a closer look. Dan was lying on the grass nearby in what appeared to be a drunken stupor. Setting the bicycle aside, Roy struggled to get him into the back of the car. Since he was a stoutish man, it was no easy task, and he finally had to give up in favour of going to get help in the shape of his father, who wasn't best pleased at being got up at such an hour. Between them they carried Dan home on a spare wooden hurdle that his father William luckily happened to have stored in an outhouse.

Verity was distraught. She had never before known Dan to get as drunk as this. Between the three of them, they contrived to get him undressed and bedded down on the sofa in the front room. Picking up his trousers and underpants, Verity threw them out through the backdoor. 'The dirty bugger has pissed himself,' she said, her voice thick with disgust.

Having advised his father to return home and get some sleep, Roy stayed up with Verity for a while. 'Dan likes his beer,' she said lamely.

Roy wanted to know how often he got drunk. 'Is this a one off?' he asked.

Verity thought it was. She hadn't seen him as bad as this before, but added in a concerned tone of voice: 'But I'm sure he's drinking more than he used to.'

'How often does he go to the pub?'

'Just Saturday nights. It's too far away from the park for him to drop in easily during his lunch hour; but he does drink beer at home, every day. I'm used to him getting tipsy of a Saturday night, but never blind drunk.'

'Is he ever violent?'

'Not what you might call really nasty violent; but he can be difficult to handle.'

'If he ever lays a hand on you, you must tell me.'

Verity looked up sharply: 'Why?'

'Because he won't do it a second time.' The menace in Roy's voice was palpable.

'No!' Verity almost shouted. 'Your not to lay a hand on him! That won't help anyone, least of all me.'

Looking away, Roy lowered his voice. 'I just don't want you hurt, that's all.'

Standing up, Verity came over to him and laid hand on his

shoulders. 'I know you don't. Now, I think you'd best go home and get some rest. I'm coming to tea next Saturday. With Jane. Remember?'

The following evening, Roy discussed Dan with Faith and Charity, who were both of the opinion that there was little that could be done. Saturday night drinking was simply a way of life that most village mothers had to get used to, unless… When Roy pressed them as to what the ***unless*** was, all they would say was for him to tell Verity to come to see them if she found she wasn't coping.

There was no dancing after tea that evening. Instead, the sisters insisted that Roy lay on the sofa with Charity supporting is head in her lap and Faith his legs in hers. Presently, as Charity stroked gently away at his hair, she said in a dreamlike tone of voice: 'What's to become of us now that our boy has fallen in love?'

'He'll leave us alone and we'll all come home,' Faith responded in an altogether brighter tone of voice.

'You mean, like sheep?'

'If you like. That's to say, if two makes a flock.'

Charity chuckled. 'Flock or not, he certainly herds us.'

Faith agreed. 'But as what? Is he a dog or a shepherd?'

Charity was adamant. 'A shepherd, certainly. He's not faithful enough to be a dog. Had it off with us both, so he has.'

Faith giggled, before drawing a deep breath and responding

in a mock-solemn tone of voice: 'And he thought I didn't know.'

Roy struggled to sit up, but Charity held him down, saying that he could have made her pregnant. Unlike, Faith, she wasn't infertile. Lifting his head and bending towards him, she kissed him on the forehead. 'You're a very lucky boy,' she said.

Roy wondered why the two of them weren't annoyed with him for falling in love with a married woman. 'I don't deserve either of you,' he said.

Faith didn't think it was a question of deserve. '***Deserve*** depends on things happening and then being assessed as to whether we deserved them or not. Happiness depends on how we handle any given situation as it comes along. Although it may well be necessary to plan ahead to a certain extent, successful living is really a matter of dealing effectively with the moment we live in. Of course, I don't deny that we may think we've failed when we've succeeded and vice-versa, but that doesn't invalidate the truth of the matter.'

Charity sighed. 'Oh Faith, I do wish you wouldn't complicate matters by getting all philosophical about them. Why don't you just say something like: having it off with Roy always seemed the right thing to do at the time. It's had a beneficial effect on all three of us. So it's good to do it.'

Agreeing with both sisters, Roy added: 'But being the best of friends and having it off together isn't the same as falling in love. A sloppy term, I freely admit, but I don't know what else to call it.'

'Never mind what to call it,' Faith advised. 'The fact is,

you have it; you're in a triangle; and these two old shag bags here must do all we can to help.'

Charity agreed adding, much to Roy's surprise, that she had a daughter. 'Two or three years younger than you. Maybe you'll meet her one day; but she doesn't know I'm her mother; so you won't know she's mine.'

Later on, as Roy walked home under the stars, he mused on the ironies of life. How could one reconcile fornication with faith and loyalty with love? He didn't know, but he was determined to find out.

The following Saturday, Dan was not long gone to catch the Ipswich bus when Charity and Jane were around with Roy at Rose Cottage. Having brought several of her teddy bears along in a small wheelbarrow, Jane asked Roy if he would make a small house for them. 'They need somewhere to live when they come to see you,' she explained, a pleading look in her bright blue eyes.

Roy explained that he would need to find some suitable wood and that would take time, but Jane would have none of it, insisting that bears lived in caves. She pointed towards the grassy bank under the ancient hedgerow at the far end of the garden. 'Like under there,' she said.

Roy reached for his spade. An hour or so later he had hollowed out a large hole in the side of the bank, which he then proceeded to line with some rocks that Verity had barrowed to him from a rockery that he had been dismantling. To prevent the roof caving in, he cut a couple of boards from a plank he had stored in his work shed and inserted them under the roof of the hole so that they were supported on the rock built walls. Then, having found an old mat to cover the floor of the 'cave', he watched with Verity whilst Jane removed her bears from the wheelbarrow and placed them inside, before crawling in herself and sitting with them.

'I should've made it bigger,' Roy said. 'She'll outgrow it in less than a year.'

Stepping up close, Verity place her right arm around him, snuggling close as she did so. 'It's big enough for the bears and that's all that matters,' she said squeezing him with her arm before adding suddenly in an notably firm tone of voice: 'I love you!'

Reaching out with his left arm, Roy held her to him. 'I'm supposed to be the first one to say that,' he said in mock admonishment.

'Then, you do?'

'Of course I do. I've loved you from the very first moment you set foot in my home. But, of course, you must have known that.'

Verity tightened her hold. 'I'm not telling you,' she said.

After a brief silence, Roy said: 'What about Dan?'

Verity was dismissive. 'What about him? You surely don't think there's anything he can do to stop me seeing you? He forsakes me - and Jane - for his football; I forsake him for Rose Cottage. What has he to complain about?'

So it was that Roy and Verity became lovers, a relationship that led to the secret of Lisa's Lodge being revealed in an unexpected fashion.

Chapter 5

Lisa's Lodge

In those days there was little that could be kept secret in a small village unless the village as a whole wished it to be kept, and this is how it was with Roy and Verity. Although it wasn't long before their neighbours became aware of their liaison and the news spread, the mentioning of it never developed into open gossip. It was a village phenomenon sometimes described as *known **of** but not known **about***. The reason for this may have been because all three persons concerned were too well liked. It might also have been because their fellow parishioners believed that it was an arrangement agreed between the three of them: Dan, Verity and Roy. Or it might simply have been that Verity was admired for continuing to behave as a good wife and mother. Whatever the reason, the plain fact was that no one ever told Dan. The fact that he might have known anyway didn't matter. It was his business and it would be bad manners to mention it unless he did. As for Roy and Verity, knowing that he knew, they weren't sure what to do about it. However, since he didn't seem to mind, they said nothing in case it complicated matters. Most important of all, there was Jane to consider. She had taken to Roy, but she was also fond of her father, which meant that there were now two father figures in her life.

It was mid June and Roy and Verity had still not committed adultery in the absolute meaning of that term. Inhibited by their concern for Jane's welfare, they had refrained from doing anything that might damage her trust in the three adults that meant most to her. If it hadn't been for Lisa's Lodge, matters may have remained in this kind of limbo for some considerable time. However, as it turned out, the whole situation was marked for change from the moment that Verity asked Roy if he had ever heard of the place; and, of course, he had, Faith and Charity having told him about it. This being so, Verity was surprised he had never been there, but Roy wasn't. There was always going to be a limit as to how much of the local landscape a resident could get to know intimately during a lifetime. Although Roy was better acquainted with his environment than most, it was hardly surprising that there were parts of it that even he had not visited.

Since it was now outside the football season, which meant that Dan wasn't away in Ipswich every other Saturday afternoon, the fortnightly visits by Verity and Jane to Rose Cottage were no longer feasible. However, this had not deterred Verity from visiting Roy, which she now did every Saturday afternoon, leaving Jane with Dan until teatime when she would return to prepare the meal and stay to look after Jane whilst Dan went to the Green Man. Whilst he was away, Roy would come across to see Verity and Jane. It was when Verity was at Rose Cottage on the second Saturday afternoon in June that she suggested that the two of them visited Lisa's Lodge sometime soon.

Roy didn't see how. 'Dan's going to have to know,' he said.

Verity agreed. 'Of course! I didn't suppose that he wouldn't have to; but why should he object? He's never taken me to task for spending time with you. Although we'd have to go on a Sunday. It's too far to get there and back during the time we have together on Saturday afternoons.'

Roy was wary. 'Dan won't like it,' he insisted.

Verity shook her head. 'You're wrong there. He's been onto me for a long time to make friends.'

'I'm sure he has, but I expect he means women friends.'

'Well, he did, naturally; but somehow he doesn't seem to mind you. Now, if it had been any other man, then I'm not so sure.'

'But why are you so sure he doesn't resent **me**?'

'Because you're different. You've always been kind to him - helped him home when he was drunk - that kind of thing. And besides, you're outside his clique. Most men, especially the ones he knows, have a coarse streak. You haven't, and he seems to sense that I'm safe with you.'

'Safe from nastiness of any kind, maybe; but sooner or later we're going to - well you know what.'

Verity chuckled. 'Maybe… Maybe; but we'll cross that bridge when we come to it. All we need to know now is that he won't object to us going to Lisa's Lodge alone together. So how about tomorrow week?'

Despite the fact that it would cause him to miss the midsummer Morris dancing festival, Roy agreed.

Dan and Jane came out to wave Roy and Verity off after an early breakfast on the appointed Sunday. Later, as they walked through the deer park on their way to make contact with the long, winding lane that led to Lisa's Lodge on the edge of Haddingham's Hollow, Roy voiced his concern that Dan was a fool to trust the two of them together. Verity disagreed. She thought he would have been a fool not to do so, her reasoning being that the risk of him losing her for good would be greatly increased should choose to restrain her in any way. Intrigued by this line of reasoning, Roy decided not to pursue the matter.

The footpath continued along beside a tall hedge on the far side of the park fence, which they negotiated by means of a set of double steps. After about half a mile they climbed over a style to find themselves in a long, green tunnel of a lane formed by the meeting of branches above them. Known as The Causeway, it ran for nearly two miles before terminating about half a mile east of Lisa's Lodge, which was as near as Roy had ever been to that place. Emerging into a water meadow, they followed a footpath leading across it and over a flat wooden bridge spanning Diddler's Brook. Crossing the bridge, they walked on through a copse, emerging in the lea of a low hill forming a ridge some distance northwards of the water meadows. They had reached Haddingham's Hollow. Pointing towards where a large clump of trees protruded from the higher ground, Verity explained that Lisa's Lodge was hidden among them. Following a track that led up alongside arable fields, the soon found themselves in among the trees. Roy gasped. He was not prepared for the sight that met his eyes. He had expected a ruin, but here was a house, highly honed and well maintained in the midst of a mini flower meadow.

'They never cut the grass till the end of June,' Verity explained in a matter of fact tone of voice that seemed singularly unsuited to the occasion.

With so many questions flooding his mind, Roy struggled to find which one to ask first. Finally, after a long pause, he said: 'But who lives here? What **is** this?'

Verity's eyes widened. 'Why, a house, of course! But no one lives here. That's to say, no one in particular. It's what you might call a staying-in house, or a meeting house.'

'You mean, a kind of holiday house?'

Verity didn't mean anything of the kind. Taking Roy by the hand, she led him over to a garden seat among the trees, where she sought to explain things to him after they were seated. A very long time ago, the last person to live in the house had been an old woman known as Lisa. After her death over a hundred years ago, ownership of the house had passed to the Rookyard family, her closest living relatives, although not so very close. It had been the current Mrs Rookyard, nee Sarah Saltworthy, who had instigated the renovation of the property just a few years ago. Sarah was friendly with both Faith and Charity and Verity knew her from having been brought up in the small village of Felsham, where Sarah's husband, Ted Rookyard, farmed and where Lisa's Lodge was situated. The name 'Saltworthy' was supposed by some to be matriarchal. Although Sarah's mother had been known as Mrs Saltworthy, no one in Felsham had ever known her husband, and it had been assumed that she was widowed when she had moved into the village as a young woman before the First World War. It was generally accepted that she had independent means and a variety of often important looking people were in the habit of visiting her isolated cottage on the edge of the village. Be that as it may, Verity had Sarah's permission to visit Lisa's Lodge. Roy wondered if they could go inside.

Standing up and producing a key from her trouser pocket, Verity bade Roy to follow her. As he followed her to the front door, he delighted in the litheness of her neat little body clad to best effect in close fitting, dark blue trousers and revealing pale blue blouse. Unlocking the front door, situated bizarrely near one corner of the frontage, she led the way into what appeared to be a small hall or ante-room, where she removed her shoes, asking Roy to remove his. Then she led the way into a large, long room with what appeared to be some kind of altar at its far end, explaining in a matter-of-fact tone of voice that this was where the Sisterhood met.

With sudden realisation, Roy exclaimed: 'Faith and Charity! They know all about your bringing me here!'

Verity threw him a coy look. 'What makes you think that?'

It was Roy's turn to be evasive. 'What makes you **say** that?'

Verity giggled. 'Play me a tune and I'll dance for you.'

'How am I going to play without a fiddle?'

'That's easily remedied. Come with me.'

Verity led the way through another door that opened into an ante-chamber where she produced a cased violin from one of the cupboards that lined the walls. Back in the large room, having tuned the violin from striking a note on a grand piano that stood at the end opposite the altar-like structure, Roy struck up a tune and Verity began to dance. Roy was impressed by the way she interpreted the music. Whatever style or tempo he choose, using feet, hands and body movements, she quickly improvised a fascinating interpretation. Having never experienced dancing quite like it, Roy was at a loss to understand how an ostensibly unsophisticated country girl was able to dance with such apparent ingenuity. However, it was when he embarked upon a wild batch of improvisations that he got his greatest surprise of all. Whirling round and stamping her feet, Verity began to strip off one garment after another beginning with her blouse and ending with her scanty knickers, which she contrived to wriggle down over the rippling delights of her bountiful buttocks to then journey with increasing speed over her inviting thighs until they fell to the ground, allowing her to step deftly from them and continue dancing completely naked. Carried away by a sense of occasion, Roy was less surprised than enchanted. What might have been sleazy in a different context, was nothing less than an inspiring work of art in this situation. Then, as he brought his fiddling to an end with a final flourish and set aside the violin, Verity ran to him and threw her arms around him. Clasping his hands around her buttocks, Roy hugged her to him and kissed her in the neck. Murmuring with delight, she held her head back, presenting her lips for him to kiss. For how long the kiss lasted, neither of them could afterwards ever remember, but it was a long time as kisses go. Roy thought that she ought to get dressed, as there was a slight chill in the air of the room. As he helped her to gather up her scattered garments, he remarked on the inviting neatness of her smallish breasts, wanting to know if she had breast fed Jane.

Verity nodded. 'Oh yes! That's why they're as you see them.

There's nothing like breast feeding for keeping a neat figure.'

Dressed again, she looked straight at Roy, telling him in clear, crisp tones: 'I want you to mate with me - soon, but not here. I'll choose the time and let myself into you with my key, and come to you in your bed in the night.'

Roy voiced alarm: 'But Dan…'

'Ssh!' Verity interrupted, a finger to her lips. 'You leave Dan to me. When I come to you, he'll not know; and that's all **you** need to know.'

Deciding it was best not to argue, Roy asked about the house and how it was used. Verity was happy to explain. It was the meeting place of the Sisterhood, used for rituals, talks and discussions. Although the rituals were performed after a religious fashion, the Sisterhood had more to do with developing matriarchy as a viable alternative to male dominated societies and religions of all kinds. Only those men who were kindly disposed to matriarchy were ever allowed to participate in any of the Sisterhoods' rituals or activities. Since such men were few and far between, no more than a handful of males had ever been allowed into Lisa's Lodge. Amazed at what he was hearing, Roy protested that, since he regarded himself as a normal male satisfied with the status quo, how could the Sisterhood have supposed that he was in any way 'one of them'?

An enigmatic smile flickered around Verity's lips as she replied: 'It's an intuitive thing. We just know. I don't know how else to explain it.'

Frowning and shaking his head, Roy retorted firmly that he had always been suspicious of intuition before adding in a slightly alarmed tone of voice: 'But us? You and me? My falling in love with you - is this all a put up job just to get me in here for this Sisterhood of yours to use me as some kind of - well, tool - to further their own ends?'

Verity's shake of the head was emphatic. 'No, certainly not! In fact, just the opposite. Our sudden love for each other was something quite unexpected. You were supposed to meet up with a single girl. In fact they had - still have - one in mind for you. I wasn't supposed to bring you here. The Sisterhood made a quick decision about it on account of - well, lets say, they know real love when it comes.'

Asking about the dancing, Roy mentioned the striptease, wanting to know if it was a normal part of the rituals.

Verity hesitated. 'Well… Depends on what you mean by normal. We certainly dance a lot, and that does involve removals of one kind and another, but not so much erotic - well, like what I did now, I mean. Fact is, this time - well, it was specially for you.'

Verity showed Roy over the rest of the house, which was equipped with bedrooms, bathrooms, a large kitchen and a dining room. As with most everywhere in that part of Suffolk, the house was connected up to both the mains electricity and a mains water supply, but not mains sewerage, which was taken care of in a large cesspit. Although all members of the Sisterhood had contributed to the cost of renovations and connections to mains supplies, a large part of these had been met by the generosity of the wealthy Rookyard family. Plans for the future included using the house as a retreat centre; hence the well equipped kitchen and bedrooms. At present it was used mainly as a meeting place for the sisterhood. It had one main drawback: the nearest cars could get to it was a car park over half a mile away at Elm Farm where the Rookyards lived. Be this as it may, Sarah Rookyard was opposed to upgrading the existing bridleway to enable vehicular access, preferring instead to provide a packhorse service to the lodge. Regarding this as a sensible ploy to increase the novelty of staying there, the rest of the Sisterhood were quickly won round to her way of thinking. Since dwellers in Felsham and nearby villages believed that the Rookyards had renovated the ruin of Lisa's Lodge as a holiday home for novelty seekers, their were few, if any, suspicions as to its true purpose. Even the extra cars sometimes seen parked at Elm Farm caused little comment. Regarded as kind hearted, affable folk, it was deemed perfectly natural for them to have a wide circle of friends. In any case, the numbers of the Sisterhood meeting at any given time was rarely large enough to require the use of more than three of four cars.

All this and more, Verity explained to Roy as she showed him round, during which it also transpired that membership of the Sisterhood was by recommendation rather than application. Women thought of as suitable candidates for membership were carefully watched and vetted over a long period of time before being tentatively approached with a view to asking them if they would like to join. Although the majority of the membership were recruited from the academia, it was thought vital that membership should be open to certain types of committed country girls, of whom Verity had been seen to be one. The sisterhood was committed to the fostering of matriarchal standards in society, whereby care for the environment would take precedence over all other considerations. The ideal behind the Sisterhood was that women should learn to regard themselves as epitomes of Mother Earth, always working for her welfare for the good of all living things. Members were encouraged to rear their offspring as true children of the earth. Sexuality was seen as something to be controlled by female needs and not something to be exploited by males for their own selfish gratification. Although it was often necessary to satiate the male sex drive, this could be done in a variety of ways without resorting to prostitution or indulging in careless promiscuity likely to result both in unwanted pregnancies and the spread of all kinds of venereal disease. Seduction was a female privilege. No self-respecting woman should allow herself to be seduced by any man.

Having finished showing Roy round and explaining things to him, Verity suggested that they make for home to be there in time for lunch. When Roy mentioned that he would be having his at his mother's, he was not prepared for Verity's response.

'Oh yes, I know all about that,' she said throwing him a coy look.

Although puzzled, Roy decided not to press the matter. After all, the incongruity of any given response could just as easily be fortuitous as enigmatic - not that he necessarily thought of it in those words, but that's what he meant. At any rate, when they arrived back at Bumber Lane, Roy was surprised when Verity said she would like a word with Mary, his mother. He was even more surprised when Jane ran out to meet them, calling out as he did so: 'Mummy! Roy! Daddy's inside, and we're all going to have dinner together.'

Having worked in his garden for a couple of hours in the late afternoon, Roy walked round to Kiln Cottage for tea with Faith and Charity, both of whom greeted him with even greater warmth than usual as they asked eagerly how he had liked Lisa's Lodge. Roy was flabbergasted. How could they have known? Then the truth dawned. Of course! They were both members of the Sisterhood. They had to be! What a fool he'd been! Faith was very apologetic. However, she also pointed out that she had given him a clue - years ago when she had once mentioned Lisa's Lodge. Still not placated, he waited until he was seated with the sisters in their front room, before glumly accusing them of using him as a plaything for their own self-gratification.

Faith burst out laughing. 'What! Don't give us that! We're your best friends and you've enjoyed every minute of it all.'

Trying hard to avoid being infected by this hilarity, Roy looked at the floor before responding with mock severity: 'Bugger all about that! I'd have been happily married by now if it hadn't been for you two.'

Faith chuckled. 'Married, maybe; but happily? I doubt it.'

Then, as Roy glanced up at Charity, he fell victim to the knowing grin creasing its way over her winsome features. Laughing with her as she began to giggle, Faith soon joined in, erupting into a peel of laughter as a prelude to tickling away at Roy for all she was worth. Escape was impossible. Charity bore down upon him, holding his arms whilst Faith deftly removed his shoes, rapidly followed by his trousers. His underpants proved more of an obstacle, but Faith was not to be denied, with the result that they, too, were soon off to reveal him well on the way to achieving a full erection. Then, as Charity administered some manual stimulation to encourage his manhood into full power, Faith jumped away to deftly slip out of her skirt followed by her knickers, which she flourished in the air before throwing them aside and declaring in no uncertain terms: 'Your mare awaits you! Stallion arise, oblige her now with all your latent power!' With that, she leaned over across the back of a nearby armchair to present her ample buttocks for his pleasure.

Now fully aroused as Charity massaged away at his firm erection, Roy contrived to rise to his feet with her along with him. Gasping with the pleasure of it all, he thought he had never seen a more exquisite sight that Faith's scintillating thighs surmounted by tantalising flashes from the whirling role of her bouncing buttocks. It was as if he were once again in the kaleidoscopic flower meadow surrounding Lisa's Lodge, the renovated presence of which promised an even greater fulfilment than that suggested by the flowers. As Charity led him to stand erect behind the waiting Faith, the scene changed yet again and he saw himself as standing before a cave of mystery protected by two great boulders. Stimulating his eagerness to enter, Charity guided him home inside the eternal cave of life where, thrusting to and fro, he finally exploded into a lingering, lust-fulfilled ecstasy.

Shortly afterwards, Roy allowed the sisters to lead him away upstairs and into the great bed that was large enough to hold all three of them with himself in the middle. They had slaked his pent up desire; it was now his turn to satisfy theirs. It wasn't difficult. Always the best of teachers, Faith had soon succeeded in perfecting the skills of a willing pupil. Hence his ability to bring them both joy and satisfaction.

Later, as the three of them lay together satiated and content, Roy asked about the relationship between love, lust and longing. Was there such a thing as 'falling in love'? What was the relationship between love and lust? Where did friendship come in, and was it more important than any of the others? Charity thought it best just to learn to accept things without asking for too many explanations, but Faith thought otherwise. For her, discovering an important truth could be orgasmic. Cheap thrills were the enemy of truth, and those seeking truth should not indulge in them. She had no time for barriers. For her, the apparent separation of art and science wasn't real. Beauty was no less a product of evolution than was function. Although, from a scientific point of view, coitus was essential, engaging in it was an art form.

Charity disagreed. 'It's just a pleasant way of getting creatures to mate so that the species doesn't die out,' she said.

Agreeing with her, Faith added: 'But there's also more to it - at least for humans. Friendship, relief, bonding - these are all part of it. Sex is not just for having babies.'

Roy agreed. 'Good shag; good gardening: that's what I say.'

Faith took his meaning at once. Happy sex and happy work went hand in hand; they fed on each other; and both could be achieved in a variety of ways. For instance, sexual desire could be channelled into creativity, although even highly creative people needed sexual relief sometimes. She asked Roy if he thought what the three of them did together was wrong in any way.

Roy didn't know. He'd never thought of it as either right or wrong. 'What's right today can be wrong tomorrow, and vice-versa,' he said.

Faith liked that. Apart from anything else, it showed that the Sisterhood had been right to choose Roy as an understanding and appreciative male. She went on to expand upon the relationship between friendship and love. 'Falling in love' was the prelude to forming a lasting relationship conducive to the rearing of offspring. Unfortunately, a man and woman could be very much in love with each other without being true friends. Marriages lasted when compatible couples fell in love and became firm friends. She saw sex between friends as being safer than sex between those infatuated with each other. Whereas good friends, devoid of blinding passions and aware of the consequences, could satisfy each other safely, the ecstasy of infatuation often led the participants into a labyrinthine world peppered with pitfalls. If Roy and Verity were bent on fulfilling their passion for each other, they should not deceive themselves as to the likely consequences.

Roy had been lucky. Spoiled by two sex hungry sisters, he had gained satisfaction without responsibility. With Verity, was his luck changing? Already a mother through her relationship with Dan, was she the right woman to become his mate and mother of their child or children? As for Faith and Charity, was their relationship with him a fulfilment of or a travesty of their Christian beliefs? Only time would provide answers to these conundrums.

Chapter 6

Triangles

The following day Roy immersed himself in his work at Ashden Hall. Nothing was ever allowed to interfere with his horticultural responsibilities. In her dissertation on love and friendship Faith had not mentioned work. Since it could be said that one was 'in love' with one's work, perhaps she should have. Be that as it may, Roy would not have understood. Since what he felt about Faith and Charity was not the same as what he felt about Verity, it was hardly surprising that he in no way supposed that what he felt about his work compromised his feelings concerning any of them. Had he taken time to think it all through, he might well have personified his gardening as Hope. There was always **hope** that weather conditions would be just right, **hope** that pests could be controlled and so on. So, if he now had three true friends, Faith, Hope and Charity, where did Verity fit in? Would she prove to be the ultimate truth in his life or his nemesis? Only time would tell.

Parson John Thurlow's problems were of a different kind. Although his responsibilities could be summed up in threefold fashion as being preaching the gospel, administering the sacraments and pastoral care of his flock, his actual concerns lay elsewhere. How did he prevent his circle of female helpers from squabbling among themselves? And how did he cope with those of them who tended to become too fond of him as a person? Fortunately for him, he had an understanding confidant in the shape of his wife Flora, who was far from being of a jealous disposition. Realising that there were certain types of women who would feel protective towards her kind natured little husband, she never begrudged him the attention he received in this way. Not being herself of an overtly religious turn of mind, her main concern was that her John should keep his job long enough for him to retire on a full church pension. Having few, if any, illusions about human nature, her fear was not that he might one day 'have a bit on the side' with another woman, but that such a woman might eventually 'shop' him to the bishop. For Flora Thurlow the so called 'sin' was not so much in 'the doing' as in 'the being found out.'

A shrewd woman, Flora Thurlow was quick to discern any hint of 'goings on' among the parishioners, and she soon had Faith 'weighed up.' Nevertheless, she liked her - a lot. Not only did she respect her for being a first rate schoolmistress, she regarded her as a well read woman with sensible ideals. Having herself come from an idealistic, agnostic background, she had married her John, not because of his beliefs, but because she loved him. His compassionate nature and winning little ways were, for her, a constant joy and something she was happy for other needful persons to experience. For Flora, happiness was something to be shared, not hidden.

For their part, Faith and Charity had grown fond of Flora. She had not seen fit to expose their proclivities as some self-righteous clergy wives may well have done, and for that they were grateful; but would she continue to turn a blind eye indefinitely? Although Faith thought so, Charity wasn't so sure. But then, she had her own agenda, as time would tell. Be that as it may, as far as Roy was concerned on that particular Monday in late June, he could not have imagined how the inter-action amongst four females, Charity, Faith, Verity and Flora was about to shape his destiny for good and all.

When Verity let herself into Roy's cottage in the early hours of the following Saturday morning, little did she realise that she was taking the first steps in that direction. Deftly removing both dressing gown and nightie, she was soon snuggling close to him, grateful for his welcoming warmth. The anxiety in his voice belied the enthusiasm of his embrace. He was sure Dan would find out. Verity thought otherwise. He was sleeping by himself in the spare bedroom, and she intended to be back home preparing the breakfast before he got up. In the unlikely event that Jane would wake up wanting her parents, she would say that, unable to sleep, she had gone out for a breath of fresh air in the balmy June night. After that, her mouth was on his, locking them into the depths of delight. Although Faith had initiated Roy into the art of the deep kiss, an accomplishment that he still, from time to time, enjoyed with her, with Verity it was different. Not better, not worse, but just different. The action, the mechanics of the business - that was the same; but not the reason behind it, and he could sense that. Even the fondling that followed it had a different purpose. Of that he was sure, although he didn't know why. There was an eagerness about the lithe vibrancy of her body that he had never before experienced. Whereas coupling with Faith was the height of ecstasy, this was a meditation.

It was then that Roy recalled the few occasions when he had coupled with Charity. If Faith was the queen of delights, then Charity was the mother of them. Whereas Faith flaunted,

Charity coaxed. Whilst Faith was mistress of a multi-faceted game, Charity was the mistress of manipulation. Verity was closer to Charity with an ethereal quality added. It was as if the need for stimulation had given way to a growing together that culminated in mutual bliss. Having been schooled by Faith to realise that it wasn't always easy for many women to achieve orgasm during coupling, Roy was surprised at how easily Verity seemed to have achieved this without his having to give extra help.

Although they drifted into sleep in each other's arms, Verity was no longer there when Roy awoke at around six thirty that morning. She was back home in her kitchen preparing Dan's breakfast. Saturday morning was deer watching time when he took a long walk in the park, keeping an eye out for anything untoward, in the shape of injury or illness, within the deer herd. He asked if Verity would be visiting Roy later that day.

She nodded. 'I always do; you know that.'

Dan peered down into his mug of tea. 'Maybe I do; but you see… Well, I like to ask - if you see what I mean…'

Stepping over to stand by him, Verity placed an arm around his shoulders. 'Yes, I **do** see what you mean. You must never doubt that.'

Reaching up to take her hand in his, Dan pressed it gently before saying wistfully: 'I'm not much good to you, am I?'

'Not much good? Oh, I wouldn't say that. You're a good father - ask Jane - and you're a good provider. Besides, I know you love me lots. It's just that…' Lost for words, Verity's voice trailed away.

Trying hard to understand, Dan attempted to supply the missing words. 'You mean, we don't spend enough time together - that kind of thing?'

'That kind of thing…' Verity echoed. 'Well, "time together" isn't always easy. People have different interests, and we must all try not to be selfish. It's just that… Well, I worry about you sometimes. I mean, like when you had too much to drink and fell off your bike.'

Dan sighed. 'I'll… I'll try to do better in future.'

Hugging him with both arms, Verity kissed him on the head. 'Don't fret. Whatever happens, I'll never leave you,' she said, and Dan believed her.

Later that same Saturday morning, after Parson Thurlow had discussed church business with Faith, he lingered, shifting uneasily, as if he had more to say. Sensing something wasn't quite right, Faith suggested that he stay for morning coffee, an invitation that he readily accepted. Charity joined them and, as the three of them sat sipping away together, Parson Thurlow, replacing his cup in its saucer, suddenly asked the sisters if they liked mysteries.

'Doesn't everyone like mysteries?' Charity retorted, eying him with an amused glint in her eyes.

Parson Thurlow nodded. 'Well yes, maybe they do. It's just that this village - well, it has such an air of mystery. I sometimes wonder if I shall ever get to know it properly.'

Charity tried to be reassuring. 'I always say that one can live in a place all one's life and never truly get to know it. I always think it's a question of taking every day as it comes. Each day brings its own mysteries. Some are solved; some aren't. But perhaps I'm not best qualified to answer. What do you think, Faith? You're the problem solver.'

Faith chuckled. 'I wish I was! What more can I say? I think you have it in a nutshell.'

Parson Thurlow attempted to explain what he really meant. There was mystery and there was **mystery**. What he meant was that Ashden was somehow different. It did things to people. 'It's as if it changes one's value judgements,' he said. 'But why should this be?'

Replacing her cup in its saucer, Faith leaned forward, looking straight into his eyes. 'Be? Why should anything be? You're here; you're accepted; the village likes you. Most of them may not attend church, but they like their parson. I hear things; I know. So, why not be content and accept things as they are?'

'Because I can't!' Parson Thurlow was emphatic. He had an enquiring mind; he needed to know. Accepting things at face value was not his pitch.

'You accept the bible,' Faith persisted.

'Who says I do? Do you take me for a fool? I question everything in it. No priest worth his salt has any other choice but to do just that. Priests are not ciphers. At least, that's the way I see it.'

Faith was impressed. 'And a very good way too; but Ashden is not the bible. However, since you persist, I will tell you one thing: Ashden is a woman's village; it is **not** run by men. But press me no more. I may've said too much already.'

Parson Thurlow's eyes glinted. 'Run by women? Well now, that could just about explain everything. I'm grateful to you and will press you no further - that I promise. Many thanks.'

Flora made a mistake. She decided to confide in Charity when it would have served her purpose better to have shared secrets with Faith. It wasn't that Charity wasn't so good at keeping secrets; she was. It was simply that she had reservations about so many things, whereas Faith had none about anything. The sponge-like ability of her mind to absorb facts stood her in good stead when it came to solving problems. Whereas Charity would contrive to find the way out of a problem as one might negotiate a labyrinth, Faith saw maze walls as either removable or negotiable obstacles. Whereas Charity could lose her way, Faith always found hers, if only by throwing convention to the four winds.

Charity invited Flora in for morning coffee. It was a hot, humid day in early July and Charity was surprised when her visitor had found her picking peas in the garden at Kiln Cottage. This was the first time Flora had called there. Flora wasn't long in coming to the point. She was concerned about John. He took everything so seriously and she was afraid he might be overdoing things.

Charity was surprised. 'But he always seems so happy,' she said.

Flora nodded. 'That's just it; he's **too** happy - if you see what I mean.'

Charity didn't. ***Too happy*** wasn't one of her concepts. 'There's so much unhappiness around; how can one be too happy?' she responded lamely.

'Well, what I mean is, if one is too happy, too content, in one's work, it's all too easy to get into a rut.' Flora was beginning to wonder if she had done the right thing to confide in Charity. Stolid she may well be, but stolidity was not necessarily the same as dependability. She was beginning wonder if Faith's vivacity might well hide a much stronger dose of the latter. Nevertheless, she ploughed on, adding that what she really meant was that her John was overdoing things and needed to take life a little less seriously. Unfortunately, since John was happy doing serious things, she had now contrived to contradict herself; but the irony was lost on Charity. Faith would have spotted it straight away. After this the conversation lapsed into banalities with Flora searching for the first opportunity to excuse herself and be on her way.

Fortunately, as she was leaving, Charity mentioned Faith. 'Shall I ask her to come to see you? This evening, perhaps? If she can spare the time, that is?'

Pausing on the doorstep, Flora thought quickly. 'Yes… Yes, please do. And… And… Well, ask her to wear one of her pretty summer dresses - if she wouldn't mind, that is.'

Turning back indoors as Flora left, Charity puzzled over the request for the pretty dress. However, Faith didn't seem at all surprised when she learned about it on her return home from school. Donning the requested garment after tea, she was only too happy to stroll round to the rectory through the balmy evening air.

Answering the front door, Parson Thurlow apologised for Flora's absence. She had decided to take the dog for a walk.

'Oh, but I thought she wanted to see me?' Faith contrived to sound surprised.

Offering a wan smile, Parson Thurlow fidgeted in a nervous fashion. 'Well, yes... Yes she did. That's to say... Well, I think it's me she really wanted you to see. But do come in. It was nice of you to come round.'

After they were comfortably seated in arm chairs opposite each other in the front room of the rectory, Parson Thurlow indulged in pleasantries for some time. So much so, in fact, that Faith was beginning to wonder if he would ever come to the point, when he finally asked if she had wondered why Flora had invited her round. Not having the faintest idea, Faith was quite taken aback when he explained it was because of himself. Flora was concerned that he was growing older without having experienced some aspects of life deeply enough. Having led a less sheltered life than he had, she felt that he was sometimes too trusting of people. An only child of a wealthy family, he had been educated at a well known all boys public school in the county. Although his parents had been disappointed at his decision to seek ordination after his having graduated from Oxford with a first class honours degree, they had sensibly done nothing to dissuade him from his choice of career. Some strange quirk of fate had caused Flora to love him from the very first time they had met each other at a house party. He had been very shy with the result that it had been her who had wooed him. She had a degree in anthropology and, since their marriage, had written several books on the subject under her maiden name of Flora Fitzgerald. Her main interest was studying the interactions among people in long established and remote rural communities. She was continually seeking to discover the precise role religion had played in the lives of country folk and also to discover how significant pre-Christian beliefs and attitudes still were in their daily lives.

Well known in academic circles, Flora wasn't, however,

much mentioned in the media, although she had, from time to time, taken part in some BBC radio programmes under her maiden name, and it was more than likely that she would eventually be asked to appear on television. Since this would mean that her true identity could no longer be concealed, she was worried that her research in rural communities would be compromised. Understanding that, Faith wanted to know if she had been asked to call because they thought that she might be able to help in some way.

Parson Thurlow nodded. 'That's right. At least, you could say that, although what you mean by "help" may not be quite what Flora has in mind.'

Adjusting herself in her chair, Faith contrived to pull the dress up a little, enabling her to cross her legs more comfortably, a posture that she didn't normally adopt without a specific purpose in mind. Not appreciating this, Parson Thurlow ploughed on regardless in response to her request for clarification.

Flora was not religious in any sense of the word. Generally regarded in academic circles as an agnostic, she was in actual fact an atheist. Strangely enough, Parson Thurlow didn't find this to be a problem. He found that he had more in common with atheists and honest doubters than he had with cocksure fundamentalists of all kinds in all walks of life. Believing in a god who had given us freewill to think things out for ourselves, he also believed that such a god would be happier with those who reached honest conclusions not to believe in 'him' than 'he' would be with those who refused to accept truth in order to believe in 'him.'

The upshot of it all was that Flora was concerned that

he was too happy and satisfied with her to be able to fully appreciate the importance of femininity in general. Hence her approach to Charity. But, for once, she had miscalculated. Realising she had been mistaken to suppose that she and the gentle natured Charity would be able to devise a plan between them to broaden her husband's experience, she had finally decided to plump for Faith's more outward going, not to say cheeky, style. Not a little intrigued as to what all this might entail, Faith sought clarification.

Parson Thurlow shifted uneasily. 'Well, it's like this… I mean, it's not easy to say. I rather think that Flora thought you might - err - enlighten me, perhaps?'

Uncrossing her legs, Faith hitched her dress up an inch or so further before re-crossing her legs in the opposite direction. She wasn't wearing any stockings. 'Legs,' she said huskily. 'Do you like legs?'

Faith could not but help notice that Parson Thurlow was blushing as he replied. 'Legs? Why yes. You see, I think I must have fallen in love with Flora's legs the very first time I set eyes on her. A tall, fine figure of a woman, she was. Still is, as you can see for yourself. But it was her legs that first drew my attention to her. She was sitting down opposite…'

'Eyes,' Faith interrupted. 'You're sure it wasn't her eyes? I mean, so many men mention the eyes, if you see what I mean.'

Parson Thurlow nodded. 'I do indeed! But no, it was her legs. I distinctly remember. It was rather silly really. I couldn't help thinking that a woman with such a fine pair of legs must have a good understanding. Such a silly pun, I know; but there it was; I really did think that…' His voice trailed away.

Uncrossing her legs and lifting her bottom from the chair, Faith hitched her dress up another inch or so before reseating herself. 'Ah, that's better. And you think that I, too, might have a good understanding?'

Parson Thurlow no longer tried to pretend he wasn't interested In her legs. Looking straight at them, he said thickly: 'Yes indeed! You see… Well, Flora thinks I've missed out. She didn't of course. That's why she's so good at it. I mean good at - you know what I mean.'

Faith nodded. 'Yes, I do. But is this wise? I mean, a man in your position - it hardly fits in with what you have to teach others; you must surely see that. And how do you think I might be able to help? I'm a headmistress. You're not the only one with a reputation to uphold.'

Parson Thurlow stood up. 'Reputation? I don't think that comes into it. The fact is, Flora's a very determined woman. I don't think either of us has much choice. It's all to do with her research - this anthropology, you know. She likes to test out all her theories. She's currently testing out the relationships between friendship, sexuality and infatuation.'

Rising to her feet, Faith gave vent to a deep sigh, before reaching down and drawing her dress up to just below the level of her knickers. 'There now! You've admired them for long enough. Why don't you step over and give them a good feel?'

Parson Thurlow hesitated. 'May I? I mean, it's awfully good of you. Fact is - yes, I really would like to do that.' He stepped towards her.

Turning her back towards him, Faith asked him to

unfasten her dress below the collar. 'I must get out of it,' she said. 'It's in the way.'

Stepping forward, Parson Thurlow paused. 'Get out of it? Yes; but not here. I'll take you upstairs to the bedroom.'

Faith was agreeably surprised at Parson Thurlow's animated performance. The little man bounced about on her voluptuousness like some small boy enjoying a new toy he had always wanted, but had been denied having until now. Initially, he had reached for a condom lying near at hand on the bedside table, but she had soon convinced him that it wasn't necessary. His performance was so animated that Faith found herself coming sooner than she might have expected as he exploded into her.

Minutes later, as they lay gasping alongside each other, Parson Thurlow explained that it had all been Flora's idea. As she was the only woman he had ever been with, she thought it was time he experienced at least one more before he was any older. Charity had been her first choice. Seeing her as a modest woman of high moral standards, she thought her to be the best choice for her shy and mild mannered little husband. Faith was amazed. How could Flora have possibly supposed that a committed churchgoer such as Charity could be open to playing such an adulterous role? Parson Thurlow, however, wasn't at all surprised. He had long since given up second guessing Flora. Anthropologists were game for anything when it came to researching into the vagaries of human relationships.

Faith was beginning to understand. At least, so she thought. 'So she choose the happy whore in preference to the dedicated dame?' she said.

Parson Thurlow was shocked. 'Oh no, you mustn't think that! She - that's to say, we - don't see you in those terms. I mean - well, you don't…'

'You mean, I don't charge for it?' There was a decided hard edge to Faith's voice as she continued. 'Now, let me put it this way: you've now had sexual intercourse with two women during your life up till now. How many men do you think I've had it off with? No, don't answer; I'll tell you: four. You're only the fourth, and I'll tell you who the other three are: Lord Denver, young Roy and with a young man I fell in love with in my youth and had hoped to wed. He was killed in France in 1944 soon after the Normandy landings.'

Faith went on to explain that maybe it was just as well that she had never married as, despite a long history of unprotected sexual intercourse with Lord Denver, she had never become pregnant. Since Lord Denver had sired five children with his wife, it obviously wasn't his fault, besides which Roy had not managed to get her pregnant. With Charity it was different. Unlike Faith, she had not been loyal to one lover in her youth and she had soon got her self pregnant by one of her several paramours when in her late teens a few years before the war. Deeply shocked, her strictly Christian parents had contrived to get the child, a baby girl, adopted by an affluent couple who had been unable to have children, but badly wanted one. After this Charity had mended her ways and had become devoutly Christian after the fashion of her parents. That is, until the advent of Roy.

Her affair with Lord Denver having been terminated by mutual consent, Faith had been on the look out for another paramour when Roy came to her notice. Having grown very fond of the boy, she had decided to initiate him into the true joys of sex. She had not foreseen that Charity would want to jump on this bandwagon. Thankfully, Roy had managed to accommodate her without getting her pregnant. Even if Charity had been young enough for motherhood to have been a sensible decision, Faith wasn't sure that she would have been the best of mothers. Life could be cruel at times. Whereas Faith the unfertile was the motherly type, Charity was too wrapped up in herself and her religion.

Parson Thurlow could understand that. He was well aware of the close relationship between sexuality and religious fervour, Saint Teresa of Avila being one of the most famous examples of this phenomenon. Or should that be *infamous*? The temptation for a priest to have affairs with members of his flock is always there and it happens much more often with impunity than without it. More than that, the more religious a female parishioner is the more likely it is to happen. Flora had a theory about it. She believed there was a connection with the matriarchal societies of long ago. Priestesses were in charge and descent was matrilineal. Priesthood being naturally the domain of the female, it was only natural that she would constantly seek to wrest it from the male grasp. Such a phenomenon was even more apparent in religions such as Roman Catholicism, in which priests were not allowed to marry. Women were feared by the Church. Hence its propensity for trying to keep them down in every possible way, both subtle and direct. The Virgin Mary had been set up as a kind of lightning conductor to channel female aspirations away from damaging the male dominated structures of the Church.

Faith asked if Parson Thurlow had always thought along those lines. He shook his head. 'No. As you may well have guessed, I've been influenced by Flora. What a woman! What an anthropologist!'

Faith liked that. 'You're very fond of her, aren't you?'

Somewhat incongruously, Parson Thurlow squeezed Faiths hand. 'I certainly am! I love her to bits!'

'And that's why you've just had it off with me?'

'Well, yes! Strange as it may seem, certainly yes!' Parson Thurlow chuckled.

Faith wanted to know what he really thought of her. He thought she was simply lovely. The sight of her sturdy thighs and well-rounded buttocks filled him with delight and her kisses were heavenly. Best of all the experience would help him develop his relationship with Flora. He would now be able to approach it with renewed zest. Pleased as she was about such an outcome, Faith couldn't help wondering if Flora had always been faithful to Parson Thurlow. That she loved him dearly, there could be no doubt; but as to the rest - well could it be that she had wanted her man to be seduced in order to assuage her own guilt at having seduced some other man.

Suddenly, Parson Thurlow said: 'All this sex stuff- it's such a strange business. I mean getting all excited, riding away and shooting spunk and all that. It's all quite daft when you come to think about it. Then, making it the fulcrum of all sinful actions - that's even dafter.'

Faith giggled. She was amused that he had used the word *spunk* in preference to the more polite *semen*. 'You don't believe in all this Adam and Eve stuff, do you?' she said.

'No, I certainly don't! And even if I ever had, living with an anthropologist would soon have knocked it out of me. Religion is so much more fun when you can see it through the eyes of an anthropologist.'

'Even when she arranges for you to have it off with a sexy headmistress?'

'Even then! In any case, I've learned not to argue with Flora.'

'But why wait so long? Why haven't you done this kind of thing before?'

'Middle age. As I tried to tell you, Flora doesn't want me to think I've missed out as I grow older.'

'So? Has it been that much different? With me, I mean?'

'Well… Both. Same and different. Same action, but different technique, if you see what I mean. With Flora - well, it's deeply satisfying. Once now, once some days or perhaps a week later, and deeply satisfying again, and again. With you, it's like a roller-coaster; thrill after thrill and wanting more as if you didn't want it to stop.'

Reaching down, Faith began fondling his balls and coaxing away at his limp penis. If it was a roller-coaster he was after, she was determined he was going to get it. Forty minutes after his first ejaculation, she was determined to bring him off again. Offering him one of her sturdy nipples, she bade him suck away at it as he rolled towards her. Seconds later, he was fully erect and feeling for her buttocks. Then, as her rubbing grew more vigorous, there was a noise in the hall below. Flora had returned from her walk with the dog. Realising who it was, Faith took no notice, but continued massaging away as if she were playing with a favourite toy. Anxious to discover how things had gone during her absence, Flora mounted the stairs. Crossing the landing and peeping in through the bedroom door, she was just in time to witness her husband's ecstasy as he ejaculated with a joyous cry. Flora gasped. As the curvaceous delights of Faith's bulging buttocks and sturdy thighs came into focus, it was as if she were herself enjoying it with her own dear man. What a wee darling of a man he was, and how grateful she was to Faith for helping her to realise how fortunate she was to have him as her husband. Having paused long enough for her husband to relax and for Faith to wipe the semen from her torso, she entered the bedroom.

Sitting up, Faith swung round to sit on the edge of the bed. Neither embarrassed nor shocked, she looked straight at Flora, addressing her as if she were a subaltern reporting to her commanding officer. 'He's ridden me just the once, but he's come twice. I decided to pleasure him for a second time on account of his having giving me such a tremendous thrill the first time.'

Stepping over to her, Flora kissed her face. 'Many thanks. I'm deeply grateful to you. He's so lacking in experience, you know. Never done it with anyone but me. I'm so glad I finally plucked up enough courage to let you do it.'

Standing up, Faith reached for her knickers, thus allowing Flora to sit on the bed beside her satiated husband. Gently flicking at his limp penis, she spoke softly, asking him if he had any left for her.

With a weak shake of the head, Parson Thurlow retorted thickly: 'Tomorrow; you'll have to wait until tomorrow.'

Leaning on her arm and bending over him, Flora kissed him gently on the forehead. 'I think I can manage to wait that long,' she murmured. 'But, I warn you, if you get too randy any time, I'll send for Faith to sort you out.'

Slipping into her dress, Faith giggled. 'You don't have to be mad to live in Ashden; but it certainly helps a lot if you are.'

Flora followed her downstairs and, as she prepared to leave, she hesitated, causing Flora to ask if there was something she wanted say. Faith nodded. 'Yes, as a matter of fact, there is. How would you like to join the Sisterhood?'

'The Sisterhood? I don't understand.'

'No, of course, you wouldn't. Are you free on this coming Friday evening? If so, perhaps you'd like to call round at Kiln Cottage, when I'll explain it all to you.'

'Sounds interesting. I'll certainly do just that.'

Chapter 7

Emma

The summer of that year wore on and Flora joined the sisterhood. Verity didn't have to; she had been a member for some time. She was also pregnant- for the second time. Roy was delighted. Convinced the child was his, he was worried about Dan. Would he know he wasn't the father, and would he mind if he did know? Be that as it may, Roy also knew that Verity would never leave Dan. Loving two men at the same time was not a problem for her. Since this was so, she didn't expect it to be a problem for either Roy or Dan.

Things came to a head when Roy told Verity he could bear it no longer. She was helping him harvest the main crop potatoes in the back garden of Rose Cottage on a mellow Saturday afternoon in mid October. Jane was out of earshot playing in the bear cave. Roy was concerned that Dan would come to realise that he wasn't the father of the expected child.

Verity shrugged. 'So what?'

Driving his large garden fork into the earth ready for another lift of potatoes, Roy paused. 'So he'll turn against you; that's what.'

Verity laughed. 'Don't talk silly. Just because Dan's the

main bread winner in our house doesn't mean he's the boss. He's good at his job, likes the football and enjoys his booze. The rest's up to me, and he'll do as I say.'

Gazing enigmatically at the rich earth, Roy slowly moved his head from side to side. 'I give up,' he said.

Verity giggled. 'And so you should. It's time you realised that it's us women who run things around here. If it pleases me to have two husbands there's not a damn thing either you or Dan can do about it. You, of all people, should know that. Or hasn't Faith got round to explaining it all to you?'

Roy looked up sharply. 'Explain what?'

Verity's eyes widened. 'Ah, I see! So she hasn't got round to it yet; but she will, she certainly will! Now, hadn't we better finish digging these taters?'

Verity gave birth to a healthy seven pound boy the following March. Dan was congratulated by all and sundry even though many people were well aware that he wasn't the child's father. As for himself, he maintained a stoical indifference as to what other folk might or might not believe. Roy was surprised, especially since Dan went out of his way to be nice to him. However, proud to be a father and knowing that he was good with children on account of his experiences with Jane, he accepted the status quo without pressing Verity to decide between himself and Dan. Verity was Verity and, if she wanted two husbands, there wasn't a thing either he or Dan could do about it. It was simply a question of, accept things as they are, or be damned.

When, a few days after the birth, Roy dropped in to see his mother Mary, he suddenly asked her to tell him the truth about Ashden. 'Although I've lived here all my life, I sometimes feel like an alien in a strange environment,' he said.

Mary smiled. 'That's perfectly normal,' she said.

'Normal? How can it be normal?'

'Because there's times when all of us can feel out of place and wonder what life's all about.'

'But it's more than that, and I think you know something you're not telling me. Sometimes I get the feeling I'm being made use of for some purpose or other I simply don't understand.'

'You're too impatient. You must learn to relax and allow time to tell its own story.' And that was all Mary was prepared to say on the matter. Refusing to be drawn further, she changed the subject.

Years passed and Verity gave birth to a third child, a girl this time. Roy was a good father. Treating Jane as his own, he thought of himself as having three children: Jane, Martin and Moira. For their part, the children treated it as perfectly normal that they should have two fathers. They didn't, of course, call them both 'Dad'. That was how they addressed Dan. Roy was known as 'Uncle Roy'. Roy was better with the discipline, probably because he was good at teaching the children all kinds of useful practical skills that required concentration to achieve effectively. If he told them not to do something because they might get hurt, they listened and learned the right way so that they wouldn't be harmed. Roy was also more patient with them than Dan. Nevertheless they loved Dan perhaps that wee bit more because he would cuddle them and tell them funny stories. They could relax with him in a fashion that was often not possible with Roy. As for Verity, she could barely conceal her constant delight at herself having two husbands and her children two fathers. Although Roy was the one she made love with the most, Dan wasn't entirely lacking in that quarter and it pleased her to pleasure him whenever he needed it. Not given to making unnecessary comparisons, she accepted them both for what they were and not as she, or anyone else, might want them to be.

John Lankester having retired some years ago, Roy was now well settled into the position of head gardener at Ashden Hall. Well aware of Roy's outstanding capabilities, Lord Denver both paid him well and saw to it that he lacked nothing in his efforts to ensure that Ashden Hall Gardens remained in the forefront of the great gardens for people to visit. Now over thirty, Roy was well on the way to being regarded as a village asset of no mean proportions. He thanked Verity for that. Had she found it impossible to make room for two men in her life, things might have been very different. As for Faith and Charity, they continued to play a prominent, if revised, role in his life. Although now both in their fifties, he still occasionally played the game of love with Faith, although Charity had grown weary of such pastimes. Had Roy not decided to pay another visit to Lisa's Lodge, matters might have meandered along in this fashion for quite a while longer.

By this time in his life Roy knew that an organisation known as The Sisterhood met in Lisa's Lodge and that Verity, Faith, Charity and Flora all belonged to it. What they got up to was another matter. As to that, all he did know was that it was not considered proper for villagers to question what went on in the lodge. After all, people did belong to secret societies, the Free Masons being a case in point, and few people bothered to try and expose their rituals. So why should Lisa's Lodge be any exception? From time to time hints were dropped that, one day, Roy might be required help out with the Sisterhood; but, so far, nothing substantial had materialised along those lines. Busy with his responsibilities at Ashden Hall Gardens, his Morris dancing, his violin playing and his home at Rose Cottage, Roy was too preoccupied to be bothered to any extent by the idiosyncrasies of what he and many others took to be the a small band of eccentric women indulging in harmless fantasies. After all, wasn't the well liked Sarah Rookyard the head of the whole enterprise? Highly respected for her charity work and high moral standards, it was taken for granted that anything she had to do with would be both worthwhile and above board. In any case, decent women such as herself were entitled to their little foibles.

Even Verity's occasional unexplained absences caused Roy little or no concern. On such occasions he was only too pleased to be asked to look after one or more of her three children - 'to help Dan out', as she put it. So it was that, had it not been for something Faith had let slip soon after the Morris dancers' May Day celebrations, the idea of paying a second visit to Lisa's Lodge may never have entered Roy's mind. It had been some while since he had visited at Kiln Cottage and she was playfully scolding him for having neglected her for so long.

'Now that I'm growing old, you don't want me any more,' she said in a voice loaded with pretence regret.

Roy slowly shook his head. 'You know something, Faith? There'll never be a time when I won't want you. Even should you die and leave me, I'll still want you. I did my apprenticeship with you, and you taught me the arts of lovemaking when I might have been wasting my efforts on messy teenage experimentation. More than that, you taught me how best to put words together, what to read to improve my education and much more besides. I owe everything to you.'

Faith raised her eyebrows. 'Everything? Surely, you exaggerate?'

Roy shook his head. 'No, not really. You're like a second mother to me…'

'Second mother?' Faith exploded. 'A mother who allows you to shag her like nobody's business?'

'You know what I mean,' Roy insisted, pressing on unfazed. 'Motherhood's a many faceted profession.'

Faith was impressed. 'You see me as a kind of professional mother? And me an old spinster! And Charity, how do you see her?'

'I don't. By the way, where is she?'

Faith looked at the floor. 'She not here. I mean… Well, if you must know, she's gone to see her daughter.'

'Her daughter? But I thought…'

'Yes, and you thought right. The girl was "farmed out" so to speak; but she's a woman now and - well, Charity did some detective work, and the upshot is, she's gone over to Felsham to see her. Sarah Rookyard arranged it all.'

Nodding his understanding, Roy didn't press the matter. The truth was, he understood more than Faith could have realised, but he didn't tell her. He had his reasons. As for now, he changed the subject. 'How about a session in the big bed?' he queried with some gusto.

Faith giggled. 'I thought you'd never ask,' she said, rising to her feet and holding out her hand.

When Verity next came to see Roy he asked her if she'd seen Sarah Rookyard recently. Of course she had, because Sarah was one of the three people she cleaned for, Roy and a woman in Ashden being the other two. With two of her children now attending school and just one to leave with her mother, she had been able to take on more work. Roy wanted to know if Sarah had anyone visiting with her. She had: a young woman. But why did Roy want to know? He pretended it was something he'd heard from one of the gardeners at the hall - a young man from Felsham, whose father worked for the Rookyards. It was rumoured that a son of the Rookyards was engaged to be married and he wondered if the girl in question was his fiancée.

Verity shook her head. 'You shouldn't listen to gossip. There's just the two sons. One's already married and the other lives away somewhere. He's a vet. He has a fiancée, but she's not this girl. Besides, she's not sleeping in the farmhouse; she staying in Lisa's Lodge.'

After an early breakfast the following Sunday Roy set off to walk across to Lisa's Lodge, having left a note on the back door in case Verity should call round. Fresh young leaves were bursting out everywhere on the trees and hedges lining the Causeway and masses of bright yellow cowslips and early purple orchids were blooming in the water meadows. It was as he was crossing the bridge over Diddler's Brook that he met her, a flaming redhead in a green dress. Her hair tumbled about her shoulders and she was wearing glasses. Tall and well proportioned, she was more than slim without seeming overweight. As Roy drew level with her, she flashed him a seductive smile, asking him if the footpath led all the way into Ashden. After he had explained that he had just come from there along the Causeway, she asked if he or any other villagers often walked that way.

Roy shook his head. 'Few, if any, ever come this far. Most are content just to walk to the end of the Causeway and back. This track runs on through land belonging to the Rookyards, who don't encourage walkers through their property.'

The woman nodded. 'Yes, I do know that; they're friends of mine. I'm staying at Lisa's Lodge. I expect you know it - or at least, of it.'

'Yes, indeed I do. Although I don't know much about it.' Roy went on to explain how Verity had once shown him over the place, adding that Faith and Charity were among his best friends.

The woman flashed him another heart-wrenching smile. 'Then you must be Roy. Charity told me about you. Allow me to introduce myself. I'm Emma Bankend. Flora Hunter, the eminent anthropologist, invited me here with a view to my joining the Sisterhood. That's how I managed to make contact with Charity, my natural mother. I'd been trying to find her for some time. I was getting close when, by a stroke of luck, I met Flora, who was able to make the final introductions. But come! I'll take you back to Lisa's Lodge. I expect you'd like to have another look round.'

As they made their leisurely way through Haddingham's Hollow, Emma indulged in further explanations. She was actually Dr Bankend PhD and held the chair for evolutionary biology at one of the leading universities. Both Sarah Rookyard and Flora Fitzgerald, better known locally as Flora Thurlow, had been after her for some time with a view to her joining the Sisterhood, something she had now decided to do. She had high hopes that Elizabeth Norton, an up and coming young anthropologist would also agree to join. Besides being a place of refuge, Lisa's Lodge was rapidly becoming a research centre for exploring the benefits of belonging to a matriarchal society as opposed to a patriarchal one. With an archaeologist among its membership, the Sisterhood was hoping to prove that matriarchy had once been the norm in most parts of the world. Emma had spent some time in the Congo, where she had studied a species closely related to chimpanzees known as bonobos. In contrast to their chimp relations, they lived in groups led by dominant females. She believed that research over the next thirty years or so would show that patriarchy was a comparatively recent development in the evolution of the human species.

As Roy listened to all of this, it began to dawn on him that he was little more than a guinea pig manipulated by a group of female idealists, who had instigated the participation of some local girls with a view to proving their theory that female domination was the norm in human society, which had been on an accelerating downward spiral ever since the dawn of the Heroic Age, when men took over. Verity, with her adept control of two men, was one of their star performers. Roy's heart sank. Pulling himself together, he asked if Emma ought to be telling him all this.

Emma's laughter peeled through the still morning air mocking the vocal efforts of a nearby song thrush. 'They haven't told you, have they? The fact is, I've been expecting you. Verity called me. Don't look so surprised! The lodge might be isolated, but it has all mod cons. She read your note, consulted with Sarah Rookyard, and it was decided that I should meet you and spill the beans, so to speak. As you may have guessed, your co-operation with the Sisterhood has been on the cards for some time. So, Mr Roy, your time has come!'

More accommodation had been built onto Lisa's Lodge and, as Emma showed him round, Roy noticed several other additions and improvements. However, the large meeting room with its grand piano and altar-like structure was still much the same as he remembered it. Emma's response to his query about a religious rite was an emphatic **no**. There was a dignified ceremony honouring the matriarchal principle and that was all. Although ritual played an important role in stimulating social harmony, it did not need to be mixed up with mumbo-jumbo in order to be effective. At least, that was the view of the Sisterhood. Those likely to hold other views were not asked to join. Faith had founded the Sisterhood with Sarah Rookyard, since which time membership had always been by invitation only.

Roy salved his astonishment by adopting a facetious approach. 'But should you have told me all this? Supposing I spill the beans?'

Emma threw him a contemptuous look. 'If the Sisterhood had had even an inkling that you would be capable of doing such a thing, you wouldn't be here with me now. But I think you know that.'

Roy nodded. 'Apart from anything else, this is Faith's pigeon. I could never, ever betray her.'

Roy thought of Verity and the children. They'd would be looking for him. He needed to make haste if he were to be home by mid day. Emma came to the rescue by offering to run him home in her car. He gratefully accepted. As they passed through Teddlethwaite on the way round to Ashden, Roy gazed wistfully at the small village school as it came into view. He wondered what her pupils and their parents would think of Faith if they knew the truth about her 'other life'. Or was it possible that some of the parents did suspect just a wee bit of what went on and liked her all the more for it? People always liked mysteries more than the solving of them. It was all right supposing, or even suspecting, that their buxom head mistress had lovers and imagining what she did with them. Knowing outright that she had them was quite another matter. Roy smiled away to himself. By opting to live out his life in Ashden he had automatically opted to live inside a delightful mystery. His joy was, and always would be, both to realise what existing mysteries concealed and in wrapping truths in more mysteries for others to solve.

When Emma stopped at Kiln Cottage, ostensibly to deliver a message from Sarah Rookyard, Roy was surprised to find Verity there with the sisters, all three of them having just returned from attending the mid morning church service. However, pulling himself together, he lost no time in upbraiding her along with Faith and Charity for having set him up as a fall guy to serve their own dubious ends.

Faith laughed him out of court. 'Calm down Roy! The truth is, you've been thoroughly spoiled by all three of us. Worse still, it continues. We're now about to spoil you something rotten by allowing you become an honorary member of our sisterhood. For selfish reasons, I have to admit; but there it is.'

Emma illuminated further. 'We need to use you as an example of how a mere male can thrive and realise his full potential in a properly run matriarchal society better than he ever could in a patriarchal one.'

'In other words, you aim to use me as a guinea pig?' Roy retorted glumly.

Verity smiled straight at him. 'And why not? Guinea pigs are delightful little creatures. You, of all people, should know that. After all, didn't you buy one for the children and make that superb des res hutch for it? So good, in fact, that we've since taking to breeding guinea pigs and selling the offspring.'

Since there was no way to deny this, Roy looked at the floor in a futile effort to stop himself from joining in with the general hilarity. The idea that he was a 'delightful little creature' after the fashion of a guinea pig was droll indeed. Seconds later, laughing along with all four women, he finally managed to say: 'Very well then, count me in; I'll be your guinea pig. I've come this far, I might as well go the whole hog.'

'The whole hog!' Verity echoed, pointing at him as she dissolved into a tear-sourcing burst of giggling hilarity.

Looking straight at Emma, Faith warned her with mock severity to be careful. 'He's laid all three of us. Watch out that he doesn't make you the fourth!'

Roy came to Emma's rescue. 'Don't listen to her! I was seduced by all three of them, and that's a fact!'

Contriving to look solemn, Emma nodded. 'So I can well imagine! But worry not! I'm in no mood to add to your burdens by adopting my seductive mode - at least, not as far as you're concerned. Now, I mean.' She blushed as she realised her mistake in adding the last three words.

It was some days later, as Roy lay awake thinking alone in his bed in Rose Cottage, that he began to wonder what it really meant to be a man. There had to be more too it than macho equals man. Team games, posturing and drinking with one's pals were not for him. Fit and healthy, he could dance, run, swim and row a boat, and turn his hand to a variety of basic craftsmanships in addition to his gardening skills. All that was man enough for him and he didn't intend to change. He liked women and preferred to choose his friends from among them, although this didn't mean he wasn't on good terms with other men. Dan was a case in point. If he could be said to have a man friend, Dan was that man. Their admiration was mutual in that they each valued what the other did for Verity, the woman they both loved. It was as if they had come to accept that a wife with two husbands and a family with two fathers was an ideal way to achieve happiness and rear children in their own best interests. Happily, the arrangement was tacit; explanations weren't necessary.Above all, Roy had come to believe that not having his children living with him all the time made him a better father. He was happy to contribute financially to their upbringing and, because they were with him only on certain occasions, he was able to devote himself to their wellbeing in a playfully educational fashion that might not have been possible under more normal circumstances.

Roy's admiration and respect for Faith was unabated. Not only had she prevented him from allowing his sex urge to drive him into an unsuitable marriage, she had also schooled him in the art of slaking it without causing unwanted pregnancies. Thanks to her advice he had not sired more than two children on Verity. More than that, Faith had also taught him the art of gaining mutual satisfaction without resort to full sexual intercourse. A happy home life was conducive to good performance at work and vice-versa. Worries, problems - they'd always be there; but he was in a better position to cope with them than most. At least, that's how he saw it. Now a third woman, in the shape of Emma, had entered his sphere of experience. That some kind of relationship with her was in the offing, he had no doubt. As to what form that relationship would take remained to be seen. Since the way he loved Faith wasn't the same as how he loved Verity, he supposed that the way he would relate to Emma wouldn't resemble his feelings for either of them. Be that as it may, he could not have conceived in his most vivid imaginings the form that this relationship was fated to adopt. As for the Sisterhood, he wasn't in the least perturbed. Accepting it as just another adventure on the pathway of life, he mused on how one could travel far without needing to visit distant lands. With this thought rolling round in his head, he presently drifted into a deep and fulfilling sleep.

Meanwhile, Emma's thought patterns had taken on an entirely different shape as she considered what came first in the process of human evolution. Did the evolution of bigger brains lead to apes learning to walk upright on two legs, or was it the ability to walk on two legs that led to the development of a larger brain? Leaning strongly towards the latter theory, she had little doubt that future discoveries would prove it to be true. Emma researches had also led her to believe that leadership among mammals was often a female prerogative.

So called 'male dominance' was often little more than a ploy to ensure mating with the most desirable females. Wolves, dogs, jackals and foxes were among the most family orientated mammals with the care of the young shared equally between the sexes, and she saw these animals as role models for better human behaviour. Hence her interest in the bonobos, whom she regarded as setting the best evolutionary example for humans to follow. Furthermore, it was her contention that early humans had done just that, and that it was only over the past four to five thousand years, since the advent of what some called 'The Heroic Age', that male dominance among humans had developed into it present form. At a personal level these views had tended to sour her relations with members of the opposite sex, resulting in her being unable to sustain a steady relationship with any man for any length of time.

Emma's discovery of her natural mother had been fortuitous. When Sarah Rookyard had first approached her to join the Sisterhood, she'd no idea about anything to do with the young woman's parentage. It was only when Emma had explained that she was adopted and that all she knew about her real mother was that she came from the part of Suffolk in which Ashden was situated that Sarah had begun to wonder, recalling that Charity had once told her that there was red hair on her mother's side. After that, with the co-operation of Emma's adoptive parents and a birth certificate, it had not taken long to arrive at the truth. The fact that Emma had met Faith and taken to her well before she knew she was her aunt was of considerable help when it came to meeting up with Charity. Since Emma liked Faith so much, she wasn't much bothered that she might not take to her natural mother. As it turned out, she did - up to a point; but she knew she would always prefer Faith.

Roy intrigued Emma. Wishing to explore him further, she hoped that the two of them could be friends without sexual feelings getting in the way. She divided manageable man-woman relationships into four main categories: One, not liking each other at all. Two, being friends. Three, being lovers but not real friends. And four, being both friends and lovers. As far as she was concerned, Roy fell into category number two. She just hoped that he would feel the same way about her. The absence of mutual feelings ruptured the four categories and was difficult to deal with. This was all very well, but Emma had failed to take into account that Roy's way of thinking might not be geared to using her kind of logic. Such an omission was not without its consequences.

Chapter 8

Conflict

Ashden was fortunate in not having been as badly effected as many other parts of East Anglia by the agricultural revolution of the nineteen sixties. Wishing, among other considerations, to preserve cover for game, Lord Denver was loath to grant permission for his tenant farmers to rip out hedgerows to create larger fields conducive to the use of combines and other modern farming machinery. When such permission was reluctantly granted, he always tried to ensure that native trees and shrubs were planting in strategic places to compensate wildlife for the loss of habitat. As for pesticides, there wasn't much he could do about them. It would be another twenty years or so before their use was properly regulated and the most dangerous ones removed from sale.

With regard to Ashden Hall Gardens, encouraged by Lord Denver, Roy had become a pioneer of organic gardening methods. He didn't see Emma again for some time. She was too busy elsewhere for her to be able to visit Lisa's Lodge more than two or three times during the course of a year. Although he thought of her often enough, he was glad not to be bothered by her in the flesh. What with his responsibilities at Ashden Hall, his music and Morris dancing and his commitment to help rear his and Verity's children, he had enough to do without being bothered by another woman. That's to say, not bothered by her in the flesh, for bother him at a distance she certainly did, even though he liked to deceive himself into believing she didn't. His feelings for Verity had nothing to do with it. He wasn't tiring of her any more than he would ever grow tired of Faith. It was simply that he had a nagging feeling that something was expected of him in relation to Emma - something that he just couldn't pin down to anything tangible. Even his requested attendance at some of the meetings of the Sisterhood at Lisa's Lodge failed to enlighten him concerning this matter. Worse still, Faith was no help at all whenever he raised the subject with her.

The reason why he was needed at the Sisterhood sessions soon became clear. Certain rituals the women had devised could not be completed satisfactorily without some male participation. Apart from some half dozen dedicated local women, the membership consisted mainly of female professionals and academics, most of them specialising in such subjects as anthropology, biology, archaeology, psychology and so on. The presence of the local women was greatly valued as a catalyst for bringing the academics back to everyday realities when they got too carried away with their various enthusiasms.

Although Roy had initially been treated as little more than a play thing for female intellectuals, he soon gained the respect of everyone for his stoical indifference in the face of any attempted denigration of his masculine dignity - whatever that meant. He wasn't sure himself. The truth was, he was at home with women of all kinds, and he wasn't going to allow any female foible to impinge upon what he regarded as a desirable state of affairs. Whatever the women wanted him to do, he tried to oblige, and if he couldn't, he said so. If a woman was annoyed at any such refusal, he accepted her disapproval without batting an eyelid. However, he was concerned that, if the Sisterhood made any further demands on his time, he would have to give up his Morris dancing in order to fit everything in.

Although none of the members of the Sisterhood could be said to be religious in the generally accepted meaning of that term, some of the rituals they followed had all the appearance of being religious rites. Lisa's Lodge had three main uses: first, as a conference centre for Sisterhood members, enabling them to share and discuss ideas concerning the development of a matriarchal society; second, as a place of retreat where individual members could accomplish such tasks such as assembling their research and writing books; and third, as a place of rest and refreshment where members could chat, go for inspirational walks and exchange ideas. As for the rituals, they were in the nature of being aesthetic relaxations of an orgasmic nature. Hence the decision to involve Roy, who had been well schooled by Faith for something like twenty years. Now in his thirty eighth year, his virility showed no sign of abating. With Faith now nearly fifty eight and Charity around sixty two, Verity was now the main fulfiller of his desires, although it has to be said that Faith continued to make demands upon him from time to time.

Parson Thurlow and Flora, both now in their sixties, were still there and it looked as if he would stay on as rector until his retirement. Much to Flora's delight, her husband's liaison with Faith, besides enhancing his interest in his pastoral duties, had also vitalised his sexual performances with her. So much so, in fact, that she and Faith became the firmest of friends. Much liked and respected in the Sisterhood, Flora had recently been elected as their president for a three year term. Delighted by this outcome, Parson Thurlow found himself running backwards and forwards between Faith and Flora like some spoiled dog angling for titbits.

By 1968 most households in Ashden had television sets, a growing number had cars and a few were beginning to holiday overseas. Owing to the popularity of Parson Thurlow, church attendance was holding up a good deal better than it was in most rural areas. Faith was a great asset in that she was devoted to maintaining the long musical tradition in Saint Mary's church. Not only did she play the organ, she trained the choir to sing unaccompanied and organised music recitals in the church from time to time. There was also a large church hall that doubled up as a hall for the whole village irrespective of anyone's religious beliefs or lack of them.

Whereas each of its neighbouring villages had a Baptist chapel in addition to an Anglican church, Saint Mary's was the only place of worship in Ashden. On the whole, unlike Norfolk, much of Suffolk had few Methodist churches, especially in rural areas. Roy, who had his own ideas about the meaning of life and death, had little time for organised religion of any kind unless it involved music recitals enabling him to participate as a violinist. Although he had grown to like Parson Thurlow well enough, he wasn't over-fond of the wee man. But with Flora it was different; he liked her. Sometimes he wondered what it would have been like to couple with her as he still did with Faith. Since she was more heavily built than Faith, her powerful thighs would likely enough present him with quite a challenge. Be that as it may, he couldn't imagine that she was ever the one on top, as Faith sometimes was with himself, when she coupled with her less than average size husband.

Faith and Roy would often enough discuss with each other the various problems involved in relationships, especially sexual ones. Faith had no doubt at all that sexuality and creativity were closely related, if not intertwined. She believed this was also true of religion. At its best, she saw it as a form of creativity or even art. It was when religion placed rules above need that it ceased to be an art form. It was all very well to rule that sexual intercourse should not be indulged in except for 'making babies', and that otherwise it should be turned into creativity. The problem was that creativity often created extra sex drive that needed to be slaked. This was where friendship came in. True friends would always find ways of helping each other out without harm to either of them.

Such was the gist of their conversion after Faith had called in at Rose Cottage to see Roy one blustery evening in late March to discuss his helping out with the music at an old time dance evening she was organising to take place in the church hall. With so many folk now committed to following the changing fashions of the pop world, she wondered for how much longer it would be possible to attract a sufficient number of people to make such events worthwhile. Roy thought this next planned event might have to be the last one. Unless they could contrive to start up some kind of folk dancing club.

Faith was game to try it. 'But who would be interested?' she asked glumly.

Roy had no idea. 'I blame the mini-skirt,' he said out of the blue.

Faith's eyes widened. 'The mini-skirt? What's that got to do with it?'

'Isn't that obvious?' Roy retorted quickly. 'It leaves nothing to the imagination. It suggests that instant pleasure is better than true happiness.'

Faith could understand that. 'You mean, it's the triumph of titillation over technology? In other words, it suggests that technique has been discarded in favour of cheap thrills. Hmm… I must say, I'm inclined to agree with you. However, from a practical point of view, the mini has been instrumental in ridding us women folk of the scourge of suspenders.'

Roy could understand that. 'But they could be rid of suspenders by always wearing trousers,' he added with some rigour.

'You like women in trousers?'

'I certainly do! Unlike the mini, they can be eye-catching without being vulgar.'

'You mean, they reveal bum beauty at its best?'

'That's right. They're figure revealing in a decent way. When women and girls are about their daily business, I like to see them dressed for what they're doing, whatever that may be, and trousers are usually the most practical things to wear for most occasions. I mean…' Lost for more words, Roy stopped speaking.

Faith came to his rescue. 'So then, it's trousers for work and suspenders for seduction? Is that what you're trying to say.'

Roy grinned. 'You've a way of putting things. If you must know, it's my opinion that stockings and suspenders are the most sexy things any woman can wear. But not for every day wear, and certainly not with short skirts. But tights are no better. So its trousers for women for most of the time with lovely flowing, long dresses for special occasions. At least, that's how I see it.'

Faith giggled. 'But you still like suspenders in the bedroom?'

Roy nodded. 'You know I do.'

By this time all Verity's children were attending school. Now aged fifteen, Jane bussed into comprehensive school five miles away, whilst Martin, nine, and Moira, seven, were both at the village primary school in Ashden. Strange as it may seem, Jane related better to Roy than she did to her father Dan. Moira was his favourite. As for Martin, he benefited from having two adult males as role models. For all three children, Dan was 'Dad' and Roy 'Uncle Roy.' Allowed to use the lake in the deer park as one of the perks of his employment, Roy taught Martin to swim and row there whenever he could on Saturday afternoons when Dan was away at football matches. He also had permission for Verity to join him there with Jane and Moira.

It never dawned on any of them that Ashden was insulating them from the real world outside. How could it when their rural idyll had its own share of everyday problems causing them, now and then, to suppose that things might be better elsewhere? Such doubts aside, deep within themselves, they believed in heaven simply because they were living in it.

Verity was a good mother. She neither worried about nor

fussed over her children. In the main, all she wanted was for them to stand up for themselves and be happy. She always tried to attend school functions to which parents were invited and she sometimes took Roy with her to stand in for Dan. Her greatest regret was that Martin could not bear Roy's surname, and she wondered if he and his sister Moira would ever come to know the identity of their real father. This was the downside of having two husbands. Otherwise she thought it to be a great idea, and couldn't understand why people who had affairs usually supposed they needed to get divorced. She was sorry for people who didn't live in small villages. What she didn't take into account was that very few villages were anything like Ashden - except possibly Felsham, where she had been born and brought up; but it was so small it barely qualified as a true village.

Although Verity sometimes went to church, she wasn't religious. She just liked singing the hymns. In any case, being Church of England wasn't the same as being religious, which was what Baptists were. Then there were Roman Catholics. She didn't know much about them except what she saw on television. The nearest Roman Catholic church she knew of was seventeen miles away in Ipswich.

Belonging to the Sisterhood gave Verity a feeling of superiority, not over other folk generally, but over the academic outsiders who also belonged to it. They'd had to be clever to get into it; she hadn't. And for all their cleverness some of them seemed to have little understanding of human nature. In particular, she disliked Charity's daughter Emma, whom she'd nicknamed 'Bonobo Bess' on account of her always running on about the sex lives of bonobo chimps. It all came to a head in July of that year when Emma decided to spend a fortnight at Lisa's Lodge writing up her latest research work with a view to publishing her findings concerning the role of female leadership in relation to bonobo social cohesion.

Now a registered charity, Lisa's Lodge had benefited greatly from the affluence of most Sisterhood members. This meant that there were now ample funds to pay the wages of a full time cleaner and caretaker. Since Verity had plenty of cleaning experience with the added advantage that she was also a member of the Sisterhood, she was the obvious choice for the job and had been duly appointed after a short consultation among the membership. Rose Cottage was the only other property that she continued to clean, and that only because she was Roy's paramour. Emma's sojourn at the lodge brought the two women into closer daily contact than Verity would have preferred.

Her head full of research data and used to being deferred to by others, Emma failed to relate to Verity on an equal footing. Although, as far as Verity was concerned, it helped that she was not expected to work regular hours, she being busier when meetings, conferences and other functions were being held at the lodge, she nevertheless needed to be there for at least a few hours on most days. Unfortunately, avoiding contact with Emma on such occasions proved less easy than she had anticipated. Realising she was there, the erudite redhead was wont to make use of her to avoid having to provide some of her own refreshments. Her patronising attitude infuriated Verity. It was such requests as 'I say my dear, would you mind terribly rustling me up a bit of lunch?' and 'If you've got time, I would love a cup of tea/coffee.' that she found particularly galling.

Matters came to a head late one bright morning when

Verity was just about ready to return home in the small car Dan and Roy had bought her between them, when Emma called through the door into the kitchen asking about lunch.

Just about to leave by the backdoor, Verity turned back, her face livid. 'Get your own bloody lunch. I'm not your servant.'

There was a poignant pause before Emma answered meekly. 'Really, my dear, I'm so sorry; I didn't realise you were about to leave.'

'About to leave, fiddlesticks! And don't you "my dear" me! In case you didn't know, I'm the caretaker here, not the sodding cook.'

'Well yes, I realise that, of course… But you're always so nice; I thought you didn't mind…'

'Well, you know what thought did! You should go and change your knickers. You've probably shit yourself when you thought you hadn't. Now, get this straight! I'm a full member of the Sisterhood on a par with all the other members. I'm not your servant - nor anyone else's, for that matter…'

Raising her hands to her chest, palms facing outwards in a gesture of surrender, Emma pleaded with Verity to calm down. 'Please! Please! I should've realised. Truly, I'm very sorry.'

Verity stamped her foot. 'Sorry! That's easy to say. The likes of you treat people like dirt and then think they can just say they're sorry and get away with it. Flora Thurlow's just as clever as you, but she treats me as an equal. Just because I'm the skivvy here doesn't mean that I'm a half wit, you know!'

'No, I'm sure it doesn't. Roy thinks you're highly

intelligent...'

'Roy? Intelligent? What the bloody hell are you talking about? What's he got to do with it? And while you're about it, you can damn well stop discussing me with him behind my back. Go back to your fucking chimps! The Sisterhood was a decent club until you came and poked your snout into everything!' Turning on her heel and slamming the door behind her, Verity marched off to her car, leaving Emma to stare, open-mouthed, at her departure.

That evening, Emma telephoned Roy at Rose Cottage asking if Verity had mentioned the matter to him. She hadn't. Roy hadn't seen her since he came home from work. So Emma spilled the beans. Roy told her she should have been more careful. Verity was a proud woman. Obviously she suspected there was something going on between Emma and himself. She needed to be reassured that there wasn't.

Having agreed in a tentative tone of voice, Emma said suddenly: 'But that's not true, is it?'

'Not true? What do you mean, not true?' Roy sounded genuinely surprised.

'I mean, not true. The absence of physical contact doesn't necessarily mean that there's no 'goings on' - as you put it.'

'Ah... Well... Yes... I see what you mean...' Roy spluttered.

'But do you? See what I mean, I mean? Look, I'm coming round to see you - right away.'

'No! I shouldn't do that, if I were you...' But Roy was too

late. Emma had replaced the receiver. He tried to call back, but there was no reply.

Seconds later, Verity came in through the back door. 'Get upstairs!' she demanded. 'I want you to shag me.'

Utterly taken aback, Roy regarded her, opened mouthed for several seconds before responding with: 'But I can't. It's not done like that - on demand, I mean.'

'Yes it is! You can't shag me because you're a bloody two-timer. That's what! And don't bother to deny it! I know it all.'

'Know it all? What **are** you talking about? And what's this "two timing"? You know that I do it with Faith, and you've never minded before; so why now?'

'Faith? What the hell has Faith got to do with it? You know damn well what I mean. It's not Faith; it's her stuck-up, prick-teasing niece that I'm talking about!'

'Verity! Please! Do try to calm down. And do try to understand: I'm not having an affair with Emma. To put it bluntly, I've never shagged her, and that's a fact.'

'Shagged her! What the bloody hell's that got to do with it? It's the mind! It's all in the mind! You shag Faith, but your minds are right. But with that red haired cow - not so! They're anything but!'

Stepping over to her, Roy enfolded her in his arms. She didn't resist. She hadn't really wanted coitus on demand; she knew it didn't work that way. She also knew that Roy hadn't done it with Emma. But she was jealous of his mind, and somehow, Emma had got into it and, she didn't know why, but that seemed worse to her than if he had coupled with her. The chances were that they never would do it together, but she wanted her out of his mind and his out of hers. Adultery was a poor way of describing infidelity. Adultery changed things, whereas infidelity didn't have to - not by a long way. Anyway, it was only a name. Relationships were only unfaithful when the various participants saw things that way. Adultery watered things down and destroyed relationships. She and Roy were a meeting of minds, and she could meet Faith in the mind, which meant that the three of them harmonised with each other. None of this was possible with Emma. She could see no way that she was going to share Roy's mind with her.

Roy took Verity into the front room and was cuddling her on the sofa when Emma arrived. Verity excused herself, saying that Dan and the children would be wondering where she had got to. Emma wanted to know how much she knew.

'Everything!' retorted Roy as he indicated an easy chair for her to sit in.

Emma frowned. 'Then, what're we to do?'

'Nothing! What is there **to** do?' Roy's relaxed tone amazed her as he continued. 'Your coming here: it mayn't have been such a good idea - at least not this evening.'

'May be not, but surely you can appreciate why I felt I had to?'

Roy refused to be drawn. 'No, not really; we hardly know each other.'

'Depends on what you mean by "knowing". There's such a

thing as the meeting of minds without the need for speech.'

'Is that what your study of bonobos has taught you?'

'Funnily enough, in a way, it has. So many of them seem to know who wants them and who doesn't.'

'And you think I want you?'

'Indubitably. I'm afraid that's the way of things. And I want you.'

'So what do we do about it?'

'Accept it and deal with it on those terms. Pretending it's not there will only make matters worse.'

Roy shook his head vigorously. 'It'll hurt Verity. I can't do that.'

'But it's a meeting of minds. We're not having an affair.'

'Precisely! Verity knows that, and she doesn't want you in my mind. It's the bonobo syndrome all over again. She knows you don't want **her** there.'

'But how absurd! Why should I in any way object to your relations with her?'

'You don't, not to the relationship, the physical one, if you like. You think it a waste of time for me to share my mind with someone like Verity. Well, I disagree. I'm not an intellectual and I'd rather share it with her than with you, and I understand her mind better than I do yours.'

Slowly shaking her head, Emma rose to her feet. 'I'm sorry, Roy, but what you ask is impossible. We're in this thing together and Verity will just have to get used to it.'

After she had gone, Roy felt like beating his head against the wall. How was he ever going to negotiate this horrific impasse when, by its very nature, no impasse was negotiable?

Chapter 9

Tragedy

Two more years went by. It was 1970, Roy was forty, his mother Mary was in her late sixties and his father was nearly ninety. It was not a happy year. Roy's father was ailing, Mary was worried, Faith had retired both from teaching and copulation and Verity was refusing to share his bed. Only his platonic relationship with Emma continued to flourish. For the first time since he was seventeen he was leading a life devoid of sexual encounters. Strangely enough, despite his pain at Verity's rejection of him, he was rather liking it that way. How long this feeling would last remained to be seen. Maybe it was a simple case of 'a change is as good as a rest' and, when the novelty wore off, he would feel lonely and deprived. Be that as it may, at a time like this, he was grateful for the companionship of his children. Only Moira was still at primary school. Martin had joined Jane at the comprehensive where she was now in the sixth form and due to sit her 'A' levels shortly. Greatly pleased with her progress, her headmaster regarded her as university material, but she had other ideas. A shy girl, she simply wanted to get herself into some rewarding kind of work in which she would not have to endure too much contact with too many people.

The way Roy's mind worked fascinated Emma, who liked

nothing better than to discuss her research work with him. She made no secret of the fact that she believed that someone with his mental capabilities was wasted as a mere gardener. Although Roy disagreed, he never argued the point with her. Since neither of them suffered from stultifying inhibitions, they were happy to discuss their sex lives with each other. Emma regarded Faith's sex strategy as a triumph of matriarchy over male chauvinism. Whereas prostitution was the result of distorting copulation and debasing it to a level that treated women as mere sex objects for the fulfilment of male lust, Faith had restored human sexual relationships to their original level where the needs of the female were always paramount.

Realising that his sexual relationships with both Faith and Verity had been led by them to fulfil their particular needs, Roy couldn't disagree with this analysis. He hadn't sought them out; they'd chosen him. However, none of this seemed to explain Verity's current attitude. Although it was likely that Emma would have a feasible explanation for Verity's behaviour, his relationship with her was the one subject Roy felt unable to discuss with the red haired biologist. Worse still, since Faith was Emma's aunt, he also held back from talking to her about it.

This impasse might have continued for much longer had it not been for two events following each other in relatively quick succession. The first of these was in the shape of yet another anthropologist called Elizabeth Norton, a protégée of Flora, whose findings she had developed into a new theory regarding the evolution of human relations. She contented that, if the Heroic Age didn't soon end, it would destroy the earth, which she saw as being in the grip of male dominated religious fervour of one kind or another. A feminist of the most virulent kind, Elizabeth hit the Sisterhood like a bombshell.

Not even its avant-garde thinking was advanced enough for her creative mind. A neat, petite, brown-eyed brunette, she made up for her lack of stature with the use of aggressive argument backed up by a deck load of stacked up data. Her uncanny methodology commanded attention. Roy liked her as much as Emma detested her.

Since the bust up between Verity and Emma at Lisa's Lodge all meaningful contact between them had ceased. Verity was therefore surprised when Emma called to see her one icy cold evening in late February. Not knowing what else to do, she invited her into the kitchen so as not to disturb the rest of the household. Emma was very agitated. Apologising profusely, she struggled to explain the reason for her visit. She was rambling on about someone called Norton. Coming to her rescue, Verity asked if she meant Elizabeth Norton, the anthropologist.

Emma nodded. 'That's right; and she's a positive cow - in fact, a bitch.'

Verity pointed to a chair. 'Look, you'd better sit down. Now, let's get this straight: she can't be both a cow and a bitch at the same time.'

Verity's humour had the desired effect. Emma sniggered. 'Look... Look, I'm sorry. You and I... Well, we really should be friends. I've no designs on Roy; you know that. It's... Well, it's a meeting of minds. Please try and understand. Anyway, I've come to ask you to - to ask you to take him back into - into your bed - if you see what I mean.'

Verity's eyes widened. 'Whatever's brought all this on? I think you'd better tell me the whole story.'

Emma did. Elizabeth, or Lusty Liz as she preferred to call her on account of her ostentatious vigour, was out to seduce Roy. She was sure of it. But she was also sure that he still loved Verity. 'Please! Please take him back!' she pleaded.

Making for the back porch, Verity reached for her overcoat. 'I'll go to him straight away!' she called back over her shoulder. Following her outside, Emma stood watching as she made her way round to the backdoor of Rose Cottage. Then, sure she had gone inside, she got into her car and drove away.

Verity made her way into the front room where Roy sat reading. He rarely watched television. Setting aside his book, he rose to his feet. 'My! This **is** a surprise!' The joyous note in his voice was unmistakable.

Going straight to him, Verity threw her arms around him. 'I've come back,' she whispered into his chest.

Cuddling up to each other on the sofa, they discussed the Sisterhood. Roy thought Emma was wrong about Lusty Liz. She had mistaken the young woman's bouncy enthusiasm for saucy enticement. He believed that Liz was a born leader with a powerful presence that belied her belittling build. She couldn't have been much more than five feet tall, but perfectly proportioned, he thought. Agreeing about that, Verity asked if he thought her attractive. Roy did, but then, he found most women attractive in some way or other. Finding people attractive didn't mean you fancied them. Anyway, saying you fancied someone was a cheap, crude way of describing emotion. Besides, there were so many ways to like people and to dislike them, and sometimes we either liked or disliked others for all the wrong reasons. For instance, we might like someone because they say nice things about us. Or we might dislike someone because they are more successful in their work than we are. Women were said to be catty with each other, especially with regard to rivalry over attracting men. However, the truth was, no balanced woman need stoop to that level. It was for her to choose her man or men, not for him or them to choose her.

Verity liked that line of reasoning. After all, had not both she and Faith chosen Roy? The plain fact was that he'd had little or no say about any of it. Lovesick swains wooing delectable damsels was a load of crap. The downside of that was men virtually demanding sex from any girl they happened to be going out with. Sadly, too many girls felt they had to give in to keep their man. This was rubbish. Any man a woman needed to do that for wasn't worth bothering about. Roy could appreciate that. Having been shy about going out with girls, he would always be eternally grateful to Faith for diverting him away from mistaking desire for love and then marrying for all the wrong reasons. Anyway, marriage wasn't what it was all about. It was how we managed our relationships that really mattered. Since Verity was a first class manager of two husbands and three children, she certainly agreed with that. She was in full control of her family, her work and her status within the Sisterhood, this last fact being the one that Emma had learned to heed to her cost. Verity's one mistake had been to be jealous of Emma's mind control over Roy. What a fool she had been to suppose that anyone could control Roy's mind! Control his sexuality? Oh yes! The women in his life certainly did that. He was a first rate example how a man could be influenced by women to play a vital role in a matriarchal society.

Roy asked about Dan. Verity loved him because he needed her and responded to her concern for him. She saw him as a victim of a male dominated society in which it was considered macho to hobnob with the boys whilst the womenfolk kept house and managed the kids. Realising she couldn't change his culture, she had wisely adapted to fit in with it without becoming subdued by it with the result that the marriage had largely succeeded on the basis of mutual respect. Until the advent of Roy, its one big problem had been Dan's lack of libido due to too much imbibing. Too much beer downing had resulted in too little cock upping. It hadn't always been that way. Unfortunately, with his sense of security strengthening as the marriage lengthened, Dan had lowered his guard to the stage where his liking for beer and football had largely replaced his need for the delights of the bedroom.

Verity had learned from the Sisterhood that morality, far from being adherence to a set of rules, was simply the best way to achieved happiness and harmony for all people. The way she saw it was that the relationship between Dan, Roy, Faith, Charity and herself was a supreme example of the efficacy of a morality that worked over a morality based on a set of rigid rules that always risked becoming nonsense when circumstances changed. Finding himself agreeing with her, Roy changed the conversation back to Lusty Liz, wanting to know if that's how she saw it all. Verity thought she did, adding that he would have to play it as it goes. Emma had got it wrong. First rate on explaining how mammalian relationships worked, she then failed to apply her findings to her own circumstances. Instead of supposing that her regard for Roy was purely intellectual, she should have honest enough to seduce him to shag her.

Roy protested: 'But you would've hated that!'

Verity was disgusted. 'Don't be silly! It's her damned dishonesty, her puerile pretence that madden me.'

'Hmm… I see! So where does that leave Lusty Liz?' Roy asked inanely.

With deliberate intent, Verity undid his trouser belt and unzipped his flies. 'Wherever you want to put her after **I've** finished with you,' she giggled.

Mary was worried about her husband William, who was now nearly ninety and ailing. He had lost a lot of weight and she doubted that even his strong constitution could sustain him for much longer if his appetite continued to decline. The hospital said it was something to do with his pancreas. It could be operated on, but it was all very difficult at his age. Anyway, William wasn't keen on hospitals. Sensing the end was nigh, he preferred to die at home in his own bed. Up until just after last Christmas, he had been able to potter round doing things such as chopping kindling, but some four weeks ago he had taken to his bed and had hardly left it since. Now, with Easter approaching, Mary wondered if the longer spring days and hopefully warmer weather would give him a fresh lease of life. She had arranged to have their bed brought downstairs to the front room to save him having to negotiate the stairs. It also enabled her to get to him sooner should he need her. He tried not to bother her unnecessarily, but sometimes he just simply needed to call for her. It was around mid morning on a bright day in mid March when Mary heard his voice making one such call: 'Mary! Mary!'

'Yes, dear! I'm coming!' she called as she hastened to the bedside. 'What's wrong?'

'Just a pain. Could you… Could you lift me up?'

'Yes dear, of course. Now! That's it! Hold onto me. There! Is that better?'

But there was no response. William had died in her arms. Realising what had happened, Mary carefully laid him back onto the pillows as the tears began to trickle slowly down her face.

The funeral was a grand occasion. The church was packed and the singing lusty. Parson Thurlow spoke well and said some thoughtful prayers including an especially moving one about going on a journey from this world. Since Faith was at school, the organ was played by an accomplished organist provided by the undertakers. She would have liked to have been there, but everyone understood. Due to retire next year, she wished William had lived until then so she could have played for him on his last day in church, but it wasn't to be.

Several days later, on a Sunday afternoon not long before Easter, Roy, seeking solace, decided to walk over to Lisa's Lodge in an attempt to relieve the melancholy brought on by his recent bereavement. Even though he and his father hadn't been all that close, he would miss the old man, if only because he shared with him a deep and lasting love for Ashden and its surrounding landscape. In this respect they had always understood each other and William had been glad that his younger son was set to see out his days in the same idyllic setting he himself had enjoyed during his long life. It was a cause of some sadness to him that his elder son Fred was virtually devoid of the sensitivities that made Roy such a dedicated countryman. Fred had taken too much after his mother, William's first wife. Roy's mother Mary was cast in a very different mould. If he could have had his time over again, he would have wished for nothing better than that she would be the mother of all his children.

Realising much of this as he walked through the Causeway, Roy found relief in his meditations as the tears trickled down his face. Some time later, on reaching the lodge, he rang the front door bell. If someone was in residence they would hopefully answer. If not he had his own key with which to gain entry. As things turned out he hadn't long to wait. The door was answered by Lusty Liz, who was staying at the lodge for the weekend to ensure some peace and quiet for her to work on a book she was writing as a follow up to her recent research into human behavioural patterns. Casually dressed in a close fitting beige jumper and dark brown slacks, she wore her hair in long pigtail that bounced about on her back as she moved about. She should have had it cut, but had allowed it to grow too long owing to her concentration on her work. Although she invited him in pleasantly enough, Roy gained the impression that she wasn't exactly over-joyed to see him. When she offered him to join her over a cup of tea, he told her to go and get on with whatever she was doing and he would make her one.

When, ten minutes later, he took a mug of tea into where she was busily typing away in one of the rooms set aside for individual members to work alone without disturbance, she turned to thank him with a bright smile, the movement causing her pigtail to swing and bounce temptingly, although it couldn't be said precisely what it was actually tempting anyone to do, if anything. For some reason loath to leave, Roy stood watching her as she took her first sip. Then, looking up, she asked him where his cup was. Momentarily lost for words, Roy pointed vaguely in the direction of the kitchen.

Elizabeth's broad smile seemed to fill the neatness of her petite features. 'Oh, don't be a silly boy, fetch it in here and join me for a chat. I could do with a break.'

Fetching his tea, Roy found a spare chair and sat down opposite her. Although she was at least ten years his junior, he felt like a small boy being interviewed by his head teacher. Again lost for words, he waited for her to say something. She asked him about his work.

'I'm the head gardener at Ashden Hall,' he retorted mechanically.

'Yes, I know that, silly boy! I heard about you at Kew. You've quite a reputation; as a gardener, I mean,' She was all smiles, and saucy ones at that, as if she were teasing him.

Pulling himself together, Roy decided to counter attack. 'And so have you, by all accounts - quite a reputation, I mean.'

Liz developed her broad smile into a bright laugh. 'Have I indeed? And for what, may I ask?'

Roy looked at the floor. 'You tell me,' he retorted in a low tone of voice.'

Liz obliged. 'I'm a bossy, self-opinionated feminist disdainful of anything even resembling male dominance. There! Will that do?'

Looking up, Roy laughed in spite of himself, as a prequel to declaring himself well satisfied with her response. 'You're what I call an honest woman,' he added with some gusto.

Liz was suddenly serious. 'But of course… I mean, I'm so sorry. You've so recently lost your father and here's me making fun of you. Please forgive me.'

Roy looked straight at her and into her dark brown eyes. 'There's nothing to forgive. I like strong women. They make it easier for men like me to get on with being creative in our chosen sphere of work.'

Liz brightened up again as she echoed: ' "Chosen sphere of work…" I like that; and so you don't mind women being in charge?'

'No; not if they have the necessary training and experience and are confident in their ability to control men in every which way.'

'There you go again: "every which way". You've a fine turn of speech for a mere head gardener on a remote country estate.'

'I've had a good teacher. Leastways, that's to say, a good teacher since I left school.'

'Ah yes, of course! You refer to founder member Faith: teacher of the tots and mentor of the mature. You've been most fortunate.'

Roy thought he could detect a note of mockery in wee woman's voice, but not being sure, he refrained from a sharp response, preferring instead to change the subject. He asked her about her work and what she hoped to achieve. In a nutshell, she put it in three words: a better world. But she was pessimistic. It would mean women taking over the leadership in several vital spheres, and men would do all they could to prevent this happening. Some women would certainly rise to high office, but they would still be little more than cogs in a vast machine dedicated to male dominance. The hierarchies of the three Abrahamic Faiths of Judaism, Christianity and Islam would leave no stone unturned to ensure that this remained the status quo, and the true voices of some of the far eastern faiths would be drowned out. Roy listened, fascinated, to her eloquent explanations, responding with an enthusiastic 'yes' when she asked him if he was on her side.

Setting his empty tea mug aside, Roy was about to rise to his feet to take hers and leave her in peace to get on with her work, when she suddenly forestalled him by jumping to her feet and skipping deftly across to him to land sideways in his lap with her arms around his neck. Planting a quick kiss on his surprised lips, she enthused: 'You're a dear, dear boy and we all love you lots.'

'Steady on... St... Steady on...' Roy stuttered. 'You must know I've enough to cope with, what with Verity and Faith, not to mention Charity. Then there's my mother. She'll be lonely now without dad...'

Liz touched a finger to his lips. 'Ssh! I know all that, and none of it means that you can't find time for me - little me, so small compared with Faith.'

Placing his arms around her, Roy allowed her to rest her head on his shoulder, her long pigtail dangling down at his side. 'There! There! Little One, I'll do my best, but I can guarantee nothing. You must know that Verity and the children must always come first, and if you're looking for someone to shag you, well I'm not sure I would want to take on anyone else. For one thing, I just think it wouldn't be right; it just wouldn't make sense.'

Liz understood that, but she wanted a friend, a real man friend and one schooled in being able to work within a matriarchal setup; and where would she find anyone else like Roy to fit those criteria.

Roy sighed. 'Oh, very well then, I'll be your friend, but don't expect miracles. I can't afford to upset Verity again - for the children's sake, if nothing else. Emma annoyed her. I can't allow any repetition of that'

Liz understood that. She also understood Emma, seeing her as a silly cow who had prostituted her natural feelings into a platonic relationship that didn't work. Verity saw through her. That's why she was angry with Roy - at least, to begin with. But, unlike Emma, Liz wasn't looking for shags then pretending she wasn't. She simply needed a male friend. If it ever transpired that she wanted to make love with him, she'd tell him so. Roy could accept that and he was sure that Verity could too, and he said so. Inwardly, however, he hoped that Liz wouldn't make too many demands on him and that she would soon find another man to satisfy her needs.

On his way home, Roy called in at Kiln Cottage where a worried looking Charity greeted him. Faith had gone to see Verity, who was worried about Dan, who had gone out soon after breakfast and hadn't returned home for lunch. Knowing that Roy had gone to Lisa's Lodge, she had first telephoned there, but he'd already left. Hastening back to Bumber Lane, Roy made his way round to the backdoor at Mousehole Cottage and into the kitchen, where he found Faith doing her best to comfort a distraught Verity. It soon transpired that Dan, concerned about an injured deer, had gone to the park see how it was faring and to decide whether or not it should be put down. Strangely enough he had come straight home from the football match the previous evening without joining his mates in the Green Man, besides which he had gone to ber early and spent some time cuddling up to Verity prior to them both falling asleep. Although in some ways pleased by this, Dan's change of habit had also disturbed her, it being so out of character for him to behave like that. Thinking quickly, Roy asked Faith to stay with Verity while he drove up to the stables at Ashden Hall, where he would saddle Kitty, the pony used for rounding up the deer when the herd needed to be culled, and ride out to try and find Dan. Should he fail, they'd be nothing for it but to contact the police; or so it seemed to him, but he didn't say that. Twenty minutes later found him cantering Kitty amongst the sturdy oaks of Ashden Deer park. It was then that he realised the enormity of the task he had set himself. It would be dark in less than two hours, an insufficient time in which to search the whole area anything like thoroughly.

After Roy had ridden to and fro and round about for some time, carefully peering into every pond and stream and examining every tree, he was about to give up in despair as dusk began to fall, when he noticed it: something dangling from an outstretched branch of an isolated oak standing stark some distance from its nearest clump of kin. Urging the weary Kitty into a canter he headed her in its direction to find out what it was. They were less than halfway there when the awful truth dawned on him. A man was hanging from the branch. Then, as they drew ever closer, his worst fears were realised: it was Dan.

Not bothering to consider whether or not he should leave him there until the police had been informed, Roy hastened to dismount with the one idea that he should get him down.

The docile Kitty waited nearby whilst he swung himself up on the end of the overhanging branch and climbed along it to get to the rope. Managing to untie it with some difficulty, he lowered Dan as carefully as he could. Then, having made ground again, he fetched Kitty with a view to loading the body onto her. Since she was no more than fifteen hands, the task was a little less onerous than it might have been. Nevertheless, it was difficult enough. Dan was a big man and without Kitty's patience in just standing there, he never would have been able to secure the body in an inverted U-shape across her back.

Roy was about to lead Kitty away with her sad burden when an idea came to him. Feeling gingerly into the side pockets of Dan's tweed jacket, he soon found what he was looking for: a note scrawled in Dan's untidily large handwriting stating the reason for his suicide - a reason that greatly surprised Roy, who wondered if Dan had confided in Verity concerning it. Be that as it may, his immediate task was to get the burdened Kitty back to Ashden Hall, from where he would need to contact the police.

Chapter 10

Jane

Dan had cancer of the pancreas. Although Verity had known about his visit to the specialist at Ipswich hospital, she had decided to say nothing until the results of the biopsy came through. They had - by post early on Saturday morning. Intercepting the letter, Dan had been devastated by its contents, Dan had said nothing to Verity. Although there was a reasonable chance that his life would be saved if he was operated on soon, he felt the risk was too great. Having decided to have one last 'night out with the boys', he made his final decision on the Sunday, using the injured deer as an excuse to visit the park. Familiar with its trees, he knew just which one to choose for his macabre purpose. As he said in his note: since he had lived all his life without hospitals, he was damned if he was going to die with one. The verdict was the usual one of 'suicide whilst the balance of the mind was disturbed', but everyone knew that was, as an ancient villager so aptly put it, 'a load of old codswallop'. Needless to say, Verity was devastated. Her best comfort was that her Dan had escaped having to endure perhaps months of suffering before the end came. She just wished it hadn't all been so sudden. Why hadn't Dan confided more in her? But deep down inside, she knew why: he hadn't wanted to risk anyone dissuading him from taking his chosen course, least of all his cherished wife.

Reasoning that the best way to help was by devoting as much of his time as possible to Martin and Moira, Roy avoided showering Verity with sympathy. But none of this helped Jane, who was badly affected by her sad loss. Fortunately, she was determined to do extra well in her 'A' levels as a memorial to her much loved dad, and this she certainly did. Parson Thurlow proved his worth, saying and doing all the right things. The funeral brought him another packed church sooner than he could have expected. The Easter holidays having not ended, Faith was at the organ. At home after the service she remarked to Charity that Dan's death had marked a watershed in the life of the village; things would never be the same again. Agreeing, Charity remarked that it was as if they had all *come of age*. Despite the apparent incongruity of the remark, Faith new exactly what she meant. Strangely enough, her biggest concern was for Roy. The resilient Verity would recover in a way that might well be beyond him. Only time would tell.

Three more years passed. The old Lord Denver, having passed on, had been succeeded by his eldest son Wilbraham, already in his fifties, whose eldest son and heir, the Right Honourable Roland, was serving as a junior officer in the Household Cavalry. Having married a year after Dan's demise, Roy and Verity now lived together with Martin and Moira in Rose Cottage. Jane had left school and now worked as a secretary in the Estate Office at Ashden Hall. Her 'A' levels were easily good enough to have taken her to university, but she had decided otherwise. A true child of the village, she was determined not to leave it. Now aged twenty one, her prospects might well have continued as *set fair* had it not been for a certain insidious fellow in the shape of Eddie Styles, the

Estate Manager, who had taken a fancy to her. Jane objected to his attentions on three main counts. First, he was around forty and married with two children. Second, she had no desire to have her love life mixed up with her working life. Third, and most important as far as she was concerned, she had not chosen him; he had chosen her. This was simply not on. She wasn't there for any man to choose. **She** was the one who did the choosing; decisions were her prerogative.

Ashden Hall was a red brick, Tudor building enclosing a courtyard itself surrounded by a moat. Access into the courtyard was via two drawbridges, one at the front and one on the north side. Each bridge led into this central courtyard through an archway in the shape of a gap in the building work with a room over the top. The drawbridges were always raised at night. The extensive hall gardens stretched southwards, well fenced from parkland on three sides with the hall to the north. Behind the hall on this side were a considerable number of out-buildings including stables, stores and workshops, all contained in a compound fenced off from the deer park. Access to the north side drawbridge was through this compound along a private, metalled road that led through the park and out into a by-road heading in a north-easterly direction from a corner of the village common land. Some of the out-buildings had been converted into offices, from which all affairs concerning the Ashden Estate were run by a small team of dedicated women answerable to Eddie Styles, whose team consisted of Jane who, as Estate Secretary, was his second in command, Penny the financial secretary and Polly the typist.

Jane very soon discovered that Eddie was imposing on her outstanding abilities to ease his own burdens of office and then taking all the credit for himself. She wouldn't have minded this so much had he not perversely sought to compensate her for this disservice, and salve his own conscience at the same time, by making up to her in a slimily amorous fashion that she found revolting. Worse still, when she refused to respond and had eventually resorted to slapping his face after he had surreptitiously pinched her bottom, he began to make her working life difficult in all kinds of insidious ways in a seeming effort to get her to look for another job. He had picked on the wrong woman. With no intention of leaving, Jane decided to consult Roy as to her best course of action.

Roy had no doubt at all that Eddie Styles could be 'brought to heel', as he put it. A plan to deal with him soon formed in this mind, but first, he advised Jane to consult with her mother Verity on getting the Sisterhood involved. Seeing Jane as a suitable candidate for election to the Sisterhood, Verity was as anxious as anyone for her to remain in the village. More than that, with her mounting experience, Jane wasn't far off being capable of stepping into Eddie Styles shoes as Estate Manager should he resign for whatever reason. Losing no time, she paid a visit to Kiln Cottage. Faith was furious. Charity advised her to telephone Sarah Rookyard right away. This was a job for the Sisterhood. Ringing round all of the local members, Sarah convened a special meeting at Lisa's Lodge for the following evening. Liz Norton, who was currently staying at the lodge, would also be included. Verity was thankful that Emma Bankend wouldn't be there. Too intelligent for her own good, her convoluted way of thinking was as likely as not to inhibit decisive action. The incisive perceptivity of Liz Norton's mind was far more likely to prove effective in the present circumstances. Having somewhat perversely taken a liking to the petite Liz, Verity had nicknamed her 'The Ferret'. If there was anything at all to be found out anywhere, she was the one to find it.

At the meeting on the following evening, Liz asked if Eddie Styles ever went walking on his own. A local woman called Judy, who lived near him, said that he certainly did - with his retriever called Bess. Liz wanted to know if he a carried a gun.

Judy shook her head. 'Oh no; he knows better than anyone that his lordship has very strict rules about shooting on the estate. He prefers to confine it to organised shoots. Only his gamekeepers are allowed to carry guns and shoot vermin at other times, and even they're limited as to what they're allowed to kill, and that doesn't include owls and hawks of any kind.'

'But does he walk in the park?'

'Yes, he does - but quite late. It can be getting dark when he returns home. At least, it has been once or twice when I've happened to notice him.'

Thinking quickly, Liz described her plan of action to the others, suggesting a team of five of the youngest and strongest Sisterhood members as the team to carry out what she had in mind. She also thought it might be a good idea for one or two older members to be there to act as lookouts and for Faith to take overall command of the enterprise.

Faith's eyebrows shot up. 'Why me? Aren't I a bit passed it?'

Liz didn't think so. 'Not in the least! You, above all, have that acute sense of hilarious naughtiness that's so vital in such endeavours. Seeing the funny side of it all from start to finish, you're not likely to become squeamish and want to hold back.'

After that, Faith found it impossible to refuse, and a plan of action was soon devised. Over the next few days, having kept a careful watch on Eddie Styles, Judy alerted the appointed team on an balmy evening in early May when she believed their enterprise stood the best chance of a successful outcome. Some half an hour later, as the randy estate manager walked with his dog through a densely wooded dale on the eastern edge of the deer park, a rude awakening awaited him in the shape of five lusty damsels bent on bringing him to heel. Hooded, firmly bra-ed and tightly trousered, they lay in wait as he entered a narrow passage through a clump of hawthorn trees. Sarah Rookyard, one of the two older women on lookout duty, had seen him coming some minutes ago, but there was no need for her to do anything. He was walking straight into the trap. All she had to do was to raise the alarm should anyone else, other than members of the Sisterhood, come onto the scene. On high ground on the far side of the trees, Verity was performing a similar service. Faith was with the younger women, directing operations.

'Now!' she hissed, and the girls moved swiftly and silently like lithe cats, four to tackle Eddie Styles and the fifth, in the shape of Liz, to take care of the dog. Styles didn't stand a chance. They had him down on his back among the deer droppings before he had time to know what had hit him. Then, as three of them held him down, the fourth reached for a pot of red paint they had brought with them. Meanwhile, some distance away, Liz held the elderly retriever by its collar. Pulling its lead from Styles' grasp, one of his captors threw it to Liz, who tied the dog to a low hawthorn branch and stepped across to assist the girl with the red paint. By this time Styles, now gagged and unable to cry out, his arms and legs immobilized by the nubile clutch of femininity, was ready for his final humiliation. Setting the paint pot and brush in readiness close by, the fourth girl assisted Liz to remove their victim's trousers and underpants. Then, bidding her colleague hold the paint pot, Liz proceeded to paint his limp accoutrements bright red, making sure to include some of the surrounding area in the process.

'Now, you lecherous bastard,' she hissed, 'Find another job, give in your notice and leave this village in peace. We're now going to keep you gagged, tie your hands behind you, burn your trousers and escort you home as night falls. The paint's been thinned and we advise the use of more thinners to help remove it. But be careful not to let your balls dangle anywhere near a naked light unless you want them burnt off.'

Shaking the rest of the thinned paint over the trousers and underpants, Liz struck a match and set light to them, as the assembled girls gave vent to a wild and derisive whoop. Standing at a safe distance, Faith clapped her hands and declared the highjack a great success. Then, having called in Sarah and Verity from their vigils, a total of seven masked females proceeded to escort their captive back to his abode with the eighth, in the shape of Liz, bringing up the rear with the leashed dog. Walking closest to Styles, Faith warned him not to go to the police. She had taken the trouble to warn the Honourable Roland, who happened to be home on leave from his regiment, and he wasn't best pleased at the lecherous harassment of Jane, whom he held in high esteem.

On reaching Styles' abode, Faith knocked at the door and gave his wife an account of what had happened to him and their reasons for so treating him, at the same time warning her not to take any legal action. The woman recognised Faith's voice and said so, but Faith just laughed, telling her that it wouldn't do her any good no matter what she knew. This was

Ashden, and it had its own way of doing things. What she didn't say was that the Sisterhood was a powerful force with influential friends in high places. When women stood together as the Sisters did, it was hard to resist them.

The following day, Styles did not turn up for work, and the Honourable Roland dropped in at the office to see Jane, telling her that her boss might be off work for several days, which meant she would be in charge for the time being. He was sure she would manage with flying colours, adding that he had already put in a good word for her with his Lordship - not that he needed to: her qualities were already highly appreciated in that quarter. As he left the office, Jane gazed after him wistfully.

When Verity told Roy about Liz Norton's role in the whole business he was very impressed. She was some woman.

Verity agreed. 'I'm glad she's your friend,' she said.

'Well, that's all she is - a friend,' he replied as if apologising.

Verity smiled knowingly. 'Yes, of course that's all, but friendship's a lot really. At least, I think so. Anyway, I like her, and I don't mind one teeny bit if the two of you...' She broke off, ostensibly lost for words, but in reality maybe indulging in a clever ploy.

Roy frowned. 'You know, it's strange how your mind works: you are wary of Emma, who's not interested in my lower region, and yet you don't mind my relationship with Liz, who is.'

Verity touched her nose with her right forefinger. 'It's

not good for you to know too much,' she said before adding rapidly: 'Liz is a very patient woman. In her place, I wouldn't have waited so long for what I wanted.'

That night the two of them made love together with additional fervour.

Since Lord Denver made sure that Eddie Styles received excellent references, he was gone by midsummer - far away to somewhere in Dorset. Sorry for him for what he had endured, his wife stood by him in the belief that the whole business had taught him a lesson he would never forget. Lord Denver was in no hurry to find a replacement. Maybe he didn't need one. He was watching to see how Jane shaped up now that she was de facto in charge.

Jane had continued to live on at Mousehole Cottage in Bumber Close after her mother Verity had married Roy and moved into Rose Cottage with him. Although Martin had moved with them, Moira had preferred to stay in Mousehole Cottage with her big sister, even though she took most of her meals in Rose Cottage. Unlike Martin, who was shaping up as a high achiever destined to leave the village, Moira was more of a mind with her older sister in hoping that she would not have to move too far away. Although not such a high achiever as her siblings, she was a very practical girl likely to find her niche in life after the fashion of her mother Verity, but unlike her in being less vivacious and more withdrawn. Even though Dan wasn't her natural father, she had always preferred him to Roy, and had been deeply distressed when he had killed himself. Martin, on the other hand, preferred Roy, who taught him the necessary practical skills as a counter-balanced to his academic achievements. Jane simply liked any man her mother liked, which meant that she had always been equally at home with both Dan and Roy. The bear cave was still there in the back garden at Rose Cottage. She had refused to let Roy destroy it, saying it would come in useful again one day.

When the cottage opposite Mousehole Cottage, known as Briar Cottage, became vacant towards the end of the summer that year, Jane endeavoured to get it let to Melanie Redgrave, a friend of hers in the Sisterhood. Hunter, the Estate Agent, had long since retired and had been replaced by another agent more amenable to letting properties to single people. Since several of his outlying properties had by now been sold off, Lord Denver preferred to let most of the remaining ones either to estate employees or to those whose qualifications were, in some way or other, beneficial to the wellbeing of his demesne. Since Melanie was an expert conservationist employed to care for the art works in Ashden Hall, he soon agreed for her to move into Briar Cottage. Jane was delighted. The pieces of her long term plan for the future were beginning to fall into place. All she needed now was for Foxhole, a third cottage in Bumber close, to become vacant for everything to be set fair for her scheme to succeed. At least, that's how she saw it and, shrewd as she was, who's to say she was wrong?

Liz liked Jane. She would try and get to see her whenever she was in the area, which had been rather more often of late. It was one such occasion on a late October evening of that year that their conversation turned to discussing Roy. Jane was quick to voice her opinion that triangles worked. At least, they had for her. She had enjoyed having two fathers, and she thought it helpful that a woman could love two men equally well at the same time. However, she was sad that so many men seemed to fail to shape up to their potentials, preferring instead to get sidetracked into a macho-world of kitsch masculinity. Most women didn't help either, preferring to play up to this synthetic world, acting according to its fake standards rather than seeking to change everything for the better.

Although Liz agreed with the gist of this, she did think that Jane was being rather too idealistic. If one were not careful, there was always the risk of losing valuable participants by expecting too much of fallible beings. Take herself, for instance. If she hadn't been so idealistic, she would have arranged it so that Roy would have shagged her long ago. Then, realising she might have made a mistake in mentioning this to his step-daughter, she began to apologise.

Jane held up a hand. 'There's no need to apologise. I quite understand. For women who see things the way we do, he's our ideal man. Hence the demand for his services. This simply goes to show that we need to find more men of his disposition.'

Liz sighed. 'But where are they? I don't know about you, but I've failed to find any.'

Jane thought for a few moments before responding suddenly with: 'Would you like me to have a word with Roy? I'm sure he would agree to mate with you if you really can't find any other suitable man.'

Liz was aghast. 'But you can't do that! He's like a father to you. Besides, what about your mother? She'll have something to say about it, I'm sure.'

Jane agreed. 'Then, better still, I'll talk to her about it. She'll know just what to do, and I think I know what she'll advise us all to do.'

'And that's to get lost, I shouldn't wonder!' retorted Liz with some gusto.

Jane shook her head. 'No, you're wrong there. My guess is she'll tell him to get on with it. She's a shrewd judge of people. More than that, sure of Roy's love for her, she has no fear of losing him. Besides, she likes you. With Emma Bankend it was different. She doesn't like pretence - acting a part - and that's what Emma did. She knows that, with you, it's a matter of what *you see is what you get*.' Jane paused before added wistfully: 'Of course, it's not easy for Emma. Charity should've been allowed to keep her and bring her up. The way they rediscovered each other was a bit of a shock for them both.'

Some days later it was Verity who told Roy he was needed at Lisa's Lodge the following Saturday afternoon. Tired of being put upon by the Sisterhood, he was about to refuse to go when she explained that his advice was needed concerning a new plan they had for the garden there for the following year. Sarah Rookyard would be there to explain what they had in mind. After that, since the matter involved his particular field of expertise, he could hardly refuse to go. But he had been deceived. It was Liz and not Sarah who greeted him on his arrival at the lodge. When she explained that Sarah had asked her to stand in for her, Roy didn't believe her and said so.

Liz Norton's eyes widened in mock surprise at the accusation. 'But why ever would I want to deceive you?'

Roy looked straight at her. 'Because this is a put up job - between you and Verity - and I've been fool enough to fall for it. What an ass I've been!'

Liz's eyes twinkled. 'An ass is it? And here's me thought you liked me! Anyway, it's true enough about the plans for the garden; but we can discuss those later - much later. First, there's a more important matter we need to address. I want you to father my child.'

Reaching for the nearest chair, Roy sat down. He had turned pale, causing Liz to regard him anxiously. Then, as she stepped forward in conciliatory mode, he held out a restraining hand as he addressed her in a hoarse whisper. 'Steady on… I need time to think this one out.'

Brushing his hand aside, Liz came and stood at his shoulder as she declared firmly: 'No you don't! You've had enough time already - both of us have. Realising that you have had a varied enough love life already, I held back hoping that I'd find someone else I could rely on, but he's never turned up. I'm into my thirties now and can't afford to wait any longer. So it has to be you.'

Roy protested. 'But I don't feel like it. Verity keeps me busy. We had it off together only last night.' He buried his head in his hands before mumbling through them: 'Oh, this is too, too much.'

Liz shook him by the shoulder. 'Wake up! It's not too much. You can do it! You may not feel like it now, but you will do before I've finished with you. And it's no use *oh dearing* about it. We've been the best of friends for some years now and I'm asking you to do it for friendship's sake. I want a child and I'm determined that you shall be its father.' Standing behind the chair, she began to massage away at his shoulders with her fingers.

Presently he said in a dreamy tone of voice: 'It mightn't take the first time.'

Bending down, Liz kissed him in the nape of the neck. 'Good! I've been wanting you to shag me for years. We've a lot of lost time to make up.' Reaching for the telephone, she rang Verity, who told her she could keep Roy there for the night.

Unfastening Roy's belt and unzipping his flies, Liz deftly drew his trousers from him and likewise his underpants. Then having slipped out of her slacks, she de-knickered herself and straddled him where he still sat in the kitchen chair, holding herself in place with her arms clasped around his neck. How different she was from both the voluptuous Faith and the sturdy Verity! Petite, yet delightfully formed, firm and squirmy, this was an entirely new experience for him. Nevertheless, she failed to rouse him; not that she had expected to, not at this stage; she could afford to wait. Suddenly, he was kissing her, his tongue exploring the inside of her mouth. Responding with equal fervour, she could feel him rising beneath her; but she wasn't ready to have him in yet. Presently, she whispered that she would take him to her bedroom. Like a lamb, he agreed, and they were soon snug together in bed, where he was soon asleep in her arms. Allowing herself to doze with him, she was happy to wait for what she knew the night would bring. It was the beginning of many such nights, all sanctioned by the inimitable Verity, and less than six weeks later, Liz knew she was pregnant. Verity was delighted, Roy was exhausted and Jane had just heard that the tenants were leaving Foxhole Cottage in Bumber Close. Although Liz wasn't an Ashden Estate employee, she was determined she would become its new tenant. Jane's neatly devised plan for the future was steadily taking shape.

Chapter 11

Roland

Aided and abetted by the Honourable Roland, Jane was able to manipulate Liz into the tenancy of Foxhole without undue difficulty. The years passed and Liz became a readily accepted Ashden resident even though her work necessitated her being frequently absent from the village. She employed a pleasant nanny called Susan to look after her little boy Jeremy. Melanie at Briar Cottage also employed Susan to look after her two year old daughter Carol during working hours. Liz, Melanie and Jane had teamed up to share the running expenses of their three cottages. They had long since accepted Susan as part of their team even though, unlike them, she wasn't a member of the Sisterhood, of which Jane was currently the most junior member, her membership having been proposed by Verity and Faith and accepted unanimously less than a year ago. Their well paid jobs enabled the three young women also to employ a part time cleaning lady and a part time jobbing gardener. Roy was always around to advise on the more technical aspects of their gardening needs, and it also helped that Melanie was a DIY enthusiast. Although Jane planned to have a child sometime, she hadn't yet decided on who its father should be and, in any case, she preferred to wait until Jeremy had started school in order to ease the burden for Susan, who would then be responsible for three children. None of the three young women was at all keen on getting married.

Now twenty five, Jane had been Estate Manager for nearly four years and a middle aged woman called Hazel Trotter had joined the team as her number two in the position of secretary. This meant that the management was now an all female affair. A little dubious at first, Lord Denver had soon grown used to it all, largely on account of the effective Jane's obvious suitability for the job. So it was that one day in the summer of 1975, the Honourable Roland, now enjoying the rank of major, walked into the estate office just before leaving off time and struck up a conversation with Jane, whom he greatly admired, but was always afraid to tell her so. They were still talking half an hour after the rest of the staff had gone home.

Glancing at the office clock, the Honourable Roland apologised: 'I say, I didn't realise how late it was. Fact is, it's such a pleasure talking to you. It's such a man to man business, if you'll excuse my use of gender.'

Jane did. 'You mean you're not bothered by my sexuality?' she ventured impishly.

His face flushing, Roland looked at the floor. 'Well, yes… I mean, no…' He stood up.

Leaving her chair, Jane moved to stand by him, murmuring into his ear: 'You're very fond of me, aren't you?'

Avoiding her gaze, he nodded helplessly. 'You're right, I really am - very. Have been some for - for a long time.'

Reaching for his right hand, Jane held it in hers. 'But you've known other women and you have someone in mind you would like to marry?'

He nodded. 'Damn it! I have to admit it; what you say is all true; but it all means so little - so little compared to knowing a real woman, and you're that - so real, so capable, so genuine.'

'You mustn't put me on a pedestal,' Jane warned. 'But you can certainly have me, but on **my** terms, and they don't include marriage. I'm willing to bear a child by you, but such a child will be reared according to my standards and not yours. I love you; I've loved you for some time, but as the man Roland, not as the heir apparent to this estate.'

Roland remonstrated that he couldn't possibly allow anything like that. She'd make him a better wife than any of the county ladies that he knew. He was sure of that. In fact, he asked her now to marry him. 'You were made to be the lady of this demesne,' he insisted.

Jane stood her ground. 'No I'm not! I'm made to bear my child by you. That's how I want it, and it'll be done my way or not at all. There's no way I can agree to become your wife and bear your heir. You must find one of your own class to do that. You may have loved me in your mind for a long time, but always remember that it's I who've chosen you and not you me. Since that's the way of it, you do it my way or not at all.'

Enfolding her in his arms, Roland murmured: 'So be it than. I'm free tomorrow night, a day before my leave expires. I'll come to you then.'

Melanie Redgrave was fair haired and focussed. Her tall, curvaceous figure was balanced by large blue eyes, sensuous lips and ample nose, all invitingly enhanced by her straight, shoulder length hair. Whereas Liz laughed in ripples, Susan giggled and Jane's laughter was voiced smiles, Melanie chuckled. Less circumspect than either Jane or Liz, she also lacked their willingness to wait for what they wanted. That's not to say she lacked patience. It was simply a case of her patience being put to other uses. For one thing, she was patient with men, but only as a ploy to get them to do as she wanted. Proficient in both judo and tai chi chu'an, she was adept at controlling all attempts at violence upon her person. Carol's father was a farmer from Teddlethwaite she had chosen to warm her bed one cold January night. A decent fellow by the name of Ted Mouser, she had seduced him into performing whatever service she required of him. Desperate at first to marry her, he worshipped the ground she walked on, as they say, although Melanie would rather he didn't. Fortunately, her moral sense prevented her from simply using his infatuation to serve her own selfish ends. Grateful that he lived up to his responsibilities as father of her child, Melanie loved him for what he was: a dear, devoted, dedicated lover, dad and darling country lad. For, although he was her senior by a dozen years or more, lad he was at heart, and would have remained his mother's boy had not the old girl died and left the door wide open for Melanie to enter, lay him flat and mother him between her legs. This was her way of doing things. Men were made to mother and those who refused to be thus used, were best shot up the arse and left to rot along the length of life's long grind. She had yet to decide if she should have another child by him. Planning too far ahead was fraught with pitfalls. She preferred to live from day to day and take her Ted in doses as she pleased. As for him, reasoning that the bond between them might be the stronger for not having been submitted to the legal process, he was initially content to play along with Melanie's plan of campaign. Employing a village woman to cook and clean for him in the farmhouse, he had resigned himself, at least for the time being, to playing the gallant lover with a paramour lodged within a rose-ringed lair lined with love and lust. And Melanie, well pleased with this arrangement, loved him for it all.

Ted Mouser was popular in Bumber Close. Jane, Verity and Liz all liked to come and chat with him whenever he was visiting with Melanie. Well off as he was and with money to spare, it was all Melanie could do to hold him back from lavishing more wealth upon her and his child than was strictly necessary. Fortunately, he soon grew used to deferring to her and settled into the relationship playing by her rules as he came to realise that, had she agreed to live at the farm with him as his wife, his happiness might well have been vastly inferior to what it now was. The success of this relationship only served to strengthen Jane's belief that it was best not to marry just for love. Bringing up children was far too serious a business to risk committing their futures to the vagaries of spousal compatibility. She saw it all in terms of: *better a visiting daddy than a doddering marriage.* And Ted was very good with little Carol. Come to that, he was also very good with Nanny Susan. Maybe he would eventually wheedle her into wedding him. So what? As long as he never reneged on his parental responsibilities, she was sure Melanie could live with that. Jealousy was for the immature. As long as Susan also realised that, all would be well. However, be that as it may, jealousy was a trap both she and Melanie were determined would never snap shut on them.

By this time Parson Thurlow had retired and he and

Flora were living Teddlethwaite in a house they had bought long ago and let out to pay the mortgage off in time for their retirement. A youngish single priest called David Doddington had been appointed rector in his place. David, who liked burning incense, preferred to be called Father David. Due to both inflation and the decline in candidates for the Christian ministry, he had been given extra parishes to look after, which meant that he was now responsible for taking services in no fewer than five churches, only two of which, including Ashden, had services every Sunday. Having taken quite a shine to him, Liz began to attend church services whenever she was at home in Bumber Close despite the fact that she was an avowed atheist. This concerned Roy, who was sure she was out to seduce the good priest, and he told her so, causing the air to echo with her rippling laughter as a prelude to her telling him she might well do that, but not before she'd born a second child by 'Randy Roy' as she was wont to call her horticultural paramour. But Roy said firmly no to that. He drew the line at having sired two children on Verity and one on Liz, beside which he always looked upon Jane as one of his. Anyway, he didn't care to be called 'randy'. He'd never sought out women; they'd always done the courting and he'd obliged; but now he was drawing a line under all that. Thinking later on what he'd said, Liz gradually became convinced that he meant it. With this in mind, she devised a cunning plan she hoped would ensure her having just one more child, of which more anon.

Mary, Faith and Charity, all now well passed retirement age, remained firm friends. Faith especially liked visiting Mary who now lived alone in Bumber Close. Of late, Mary had become increasingly concerned about developments among her neighbours, which she thought were beginning to get out of hand. It was all very well for women to be in control, but that didn't have to mean that conventional marriage had to be ditched out of hand. As always, Faith was more philosophical about the matter. Her view was that, left to itself, a river would always find the best way of reaching the sea. If necessary, it would change course, creating an oxbow. For the time being, Melanie, Liz and Jane, guided by their own moral zeitgeist, were forging ahead with flying colours along their chosen route, which was working for them. So why would anyone want to worry about changing their obviously successful life style? In any case, should they encounter any insurmountable obstacle, they could always create an oxbow. So why worry? In any case, they were doing society a service by trying out a fresh way of doing things to see if it worked.

Mary sighed. 'Ah well... I suppose you're right. There's a deal of truth in the old adage: *nothing ventured, nothing gained*. After all, I'm the last one to be moralising about others. The plan you and I devised for the breaking in of Roy was anything but conventional. What mother anywhere would collude with another mature woman to initiate her son into the art of sexual encounters?'

Faith looked at the floor. 'I just hope I made a good job of it, that's all.'

Mary believed she had, adding: 'None of us could've foreseen that he would fall for a married woman. But even there, as it turned out, it was all for the best. To everyone's benefit, luck intervened and Dan played along with it all - and would be doing so yet had it not been for his need to make a tragic choice. As for this business with Liz, that's Verity's pigeon.'

Faith agreed: 'That's right, and more than that, it all goes to show that the Sisterhood works. Verity agrees to loan Roy to Liz, who can't find anyone better to father her child, and all is well. Not once has Roy run after any girl or woman. It's always been us who've chosen him, and that's how it should be. Best of all, we all love him.'

Glancing wistfully across at her, Mary said: 'You love him a lot, don't you?'

Faith nodded. 'He's the love of my life. Boy, pupil, lover, brother, friend - he's been all those to me and more - and still is, for that matter.'

Standing up, Mary went too look out of the window. 'I'm sure he thinks the same way about you.'

Faith stepped over and placed an arm around Mary's shoulders. 'How can you possibly know that?'she said, her voice barely above a whisper.

Patting Faith's hand, Mary retorted: 'Because I'm his mother. You and me: he loves us both because we give him the reason for his being here. He loves Verity because she gives his children the reason for their being here. He's the brilliant father he is because of us. Judge for yourself, which one he's going to love the most in the general sense of all love and not just falling in love. And it has to be you even more than me because you could do something for him I couldn't.'

Overwhelmed by Mary's appreciation, Faith was silent for several moments before responding. 'Teaching's my vocation, and I thank God it's not limited to the time spent in school teaching five to eleven year olds.'

The Honourable Roland decided to walk to Mousehole Cottage so as to avoid his car being seen parked outside it during the night. Having arranged for Moira to spend the night with Roy and Verity, Jane was all alone. Sensing right away that he was ill at ease, she seated him in the front room and asked if he'd like something to drink. Although he was desperate for a stiff whisky, he shook his head, saying he required nothing. Wishing to give him time to compose himself, Jane sat down opposite him with a view to engaging him in general conversation in an attempt to restore his confidence. However, finding this was no easy task, she soon adopted a more direct approach by asking him if he found making love with a woman difficult.

Looking at the floor, Roland nodded. 'I suppose I do. That's to say…'

'You mean, it's difficult with someone you're in love with?' Jane prompted.

'Well, yes, I suppose that's right. You see, I've never…' Again he paused.

'You mean, you've never done it for love?' Jane pressed him.

Suddenly, he looked up and straight at her. 'That's right. Look, you might s well know the truth. I've only ever done it with - well call girls - in fact, one in particular - mostly, that is.'

'And you're fond of her? I mean, the one you do it most with?'

'Heavens no! I mean… Well, I like her a lot and all that, but only because… because she's… she's…'

'You mean, because she's a good performer?'

'Maybe. Look, I don't know. I mean, I didn't want you to know. It's all… Well, it's all so…'

'Sordid? Is that the word you're looking for? And you're worried that all sex might be the same? All sordid, that is?'

Roland avoided her gaze. 'Something like that, yes. You see, it's like defiling something you hold very dear.'

Jane raised her eyebrows. 'Something? Anyway, we'll let that pass.' She stood up. 'Maybe this was all a big mistake.'

Rising to his feet, Roland stepped close up to her. 'Oh no, please don't say that! You're so lovely, so understanding. Please don't reject me. You know that my greatest desire is to have you for my wife and mother to my heir. But, if that can't be, I want to do all I can to please the woman I love.'

Placing her arms around him and pinioning his to his sides, Jane held her face close to his as she whispered: 'Then you'd better get on with doing it, hadn't you?' Loosing her hold, she took him by the hand. 'Now, come with me and I'll take you through it step by step.' She led him from the room as if he were a young boy she was about to teach how to use a washing machine for the first time.

Once in her bedroom, Jane proceeded to help Roland undress before settling his naked form snugly under the bed covers, from where she bade him watch her. Then, as she began slowly to disrobe, she asked him what it was he liked best about a woman. Happy, he liked them to be happy. So many women were never satisfied, always moaning about something, finding fault and wanting more. And the way they did it was even worse. It was all so pretentious, overblown and tiresome. They wanted you to think that they cared, which was why they criticised. They wanted things done better; that's why they were dissatisfied, *and not because it gave them a sense of superiority to talk like that.* Thus did they deceive themselves.

Unfastening her bra, Jane leaned forward, slipping it down over her shoulders, contriving as she did do to arrange her breasts so as to aim their inviting pink nipples temptingly towards him. Then, wriggling seductively out of her knickers, she turned to present the glory of her ample buttocks for his inspection. As all chivalrous inhibitions fled his mind, he rapidly rose to the occasion with a gasp of unbridled lust. Giving him no time to recover, Jane pulled back the bed clothes, leaned over him and squeezed his erection between her breasts. Then, moving astride him, she remained upright as she contrived to impale herself on his erect penis, before moving down to lie astride to begin joining her mouth to his as he began thrusting upwards to keep connected. Pausing for a few moments, she asked him how she compared with his call girl doxy. Carried away by her sheer physical conquest of him, there was no need for him to reply. He had learned his first lesson: being desperately in love with a woman didn't mean that a man couldn't still lust after her as physically as he might after lust after any attractive female anywhere. Thrillingly successful copulation could be reached by a number of routes; falling in love with each other was just one of them. This was equally true of unsatisfactory copulation; being in love with each other was no guarantee of its success. It was well for Roland that Jane had been well schooled by the Sisterhood in lovemaking techniques, which could be summed up by the three 'C's': compassion, caution and carefree abandon. The participants had to care for and respect each other, they needed to take all necessary health and other precautions and they needed to be carefree in seeking for each other's fulfilment. Had not Jane adhered to this code of practice, his performance might have fallen well short of what he had achieved with his high class whore. As it turned out, before the night was out, she had drained his well dry. Nevertheless, she was up and away to work, her usual bright self, well before nine o'clock the following morning, leaving him to languish over a late breakfast before walking back to Ashden Hall to prepare for his return to his regiment.

As the weeks passed and Jane knew she was pregnant, she was glad that she would never wed Roland. Apart from the fact that she wasn't cut out to become ladyship to any lord, she wasn't sure that her love for him was insulated against the weakness of waning as the years passed. Although she loved him now as a *dear, lost boy,* would she still love him if and when he became a *well-heeled lord*? Rather, she had seduced him because she wanted his child for her own good reasons - reasons that only time would reveal.

Chapter 12

Father David

Over a year had passed and Liz had called at the rectory to consult with Father David concerning the service of nine lessons and carols due to take place in Saint Mary's Church in a few weeks time. Having run across her during one of her erratic visits to the village, he had asked if she would read one of the lessons on that occasion. Knowing she would be at home that weekend, she had foolishly agreed to do so. However, having had time to reflect, she didn't think it appropriate that a non believer such as herself ought to be doing anything of that kind, and she told him so.

Father David was nonplussed. 'A non-believer? But every Sunday you're at home you never miss attending church!'

Her petite form ensconced in a large armchair that didn't allow for her feet to touch ground, Liz shifted uneasily. 'Well... Look, the truth is, I didn't want you to know that - not before this, I mean.'

From his own position in a matching arm chair on the opposite side of the hearth in the rectory drawing room, Father David voiced his bewilderment. 'Didn't want me to know? Agreed to read a lesson and now don't want to? What is all this? Am I missing something here? I mean, perhaps you could be a little more specific?'

Liz screwed up her mouth in a fruitless effort to find the right words, but all she could think of was how vulnerable he looked, this quaint wee man with his serious, thin face, bisected incongruously by such sensuous lips, and dominated by such piercingly frank eyes, belying their pale blue hue, below his broad forehead beneath a receding hairline. Presently, she said: 'Well, the fact is, I like you a lot. That's to say, very much.'

'Very kind of you to say so; but I fail to see the connection between liking me and not wanting to read the lesson,' Father David retorted in an entirely level, unemotional tone of voice.

'Connection? Oh, I see! Well, of course, you wouldn't. How could you?' Liz said before pausing and drawing a deep breath before suddenly exclaiming: 'I suppose you think I attend church to worship God?'

Father David's eyes widened. 'Why yes, indeed, something of that sort had crossed my mind.'

Enraged by his matter of fact tone of voice, Liz erupted. 'Well, you needn't be so damned smug about it. I come to your bloody church because I'm besotted with you, agree to read a lesson about some mythological crap that never happened and support your fucking church with my hard earned cash and all you can say is "something of that sort had crossed my mind." And, anyway, this bloody chair's too big. You might have had the decency to show me to one that fitted me.'

Holding up his hands, Father David pleaded for sanity. 'Please! Please! Now, what's this all about? If I'm not mistaken, there's a deal more to it than changing your mind about reading a lesson. Would you like to be more specific?'

Contriving to extricate herself form the arms of the oversize chair, Liz struggled to her feet to stand, stamping her rage before the unfazed priest. 'Be more specific? I'll give specific, you cold, fish-hearted fart of a would be friar! You're nothing more than a sanctimonious cipher fed by the falsities of a fairyland fantasy.'

Rising to his feet, Father David stood meekly before her, speaking in a matter-of-fact tone of voice. 'Thanks for the alliteration; it's greatly appreciated.'

Liz slapped his face. 'You bastard! Are you utterly devoid of feeling?'

Father David stepped closer. Although he wasn't tall he was still able to look down into the fury of her distorted features. Then, taking her hands firmly in his, he said in a carefully enunciated, level tone of voice: 'I'm afraid I can't ask you to marry me right at this moment; such an important step requires careful consideration.'

Avoiding his gaze, Liz smothered a desire to laugh in a fatalistic snigger. 'The answer's… the answer's yes anyway. And let go my hands. Are you afraid I'm going to rip the pants off you or something.'

Father David kissed her gently on the forehead. 'Some such thought had crossed my mind,' he said in a nonchalant tone of voice before adding whimsically: 'More importantly: are you or are you not going to read the lesson at the service?'

Gazing straight up into his eyes, Liz mimicked: 'I'm

afraid I can't tell you right at this moment; such an important decision requires careful consideration.'

The following day Father David called in at Kiln Cottage to see Faith and Charity, whose views on a variety of matters he greatly valued. When he informed them that he was thinking of resigning and quitting the ministry of the church, they were amazed, and when they heard that it was because he was thinking of getting married, they were flabbergasted. Faith protested that marriage was no obstacle to his functioning as their priest. He might be high church, but he wasn't an RC.

Father David came straight to the point. 'I'm going to ask Liz Norton to marry me. She's a non-believer with an illegitimate child. Although the bishop can't stop me, I've a feeling that he won't approve. As difficult as that is, I might easily disregard it if it wasn't for something else...' Father David hesitated.

'And that is?' Faith prompted.

'Well, let me put it this way: there seems to be some kind of... well, female conspiracy going on around here that it's difficult to pinpoint, but I know something of the kind is there. As to its influence, I wouldn't care to judge it in terms of right and wrong. All I know is that Liz is involved and, if I were to wed her, I couldn't also fail to be involved if only by association. The problem is, although I'm not prepared to pass any judgements, the wider church authorities might well do so, especially if, as I believe, they conclude that what is going on is contrary to the Church's teaching concerning sex and marriage...' Pausing, Father David sighed.

Twenty minutes later, Faith and Charity had persuaded

him to change his mind. Why bother to wed? Why not simply sleep with Liz and even get her with child? After all, that's what she wanted: for him to father her child. No one would ever know. Liz would certainly never shop him to the bishop - or to anyone else for that matter. That wasn't the way things were done in Ashden. Its church was dedicated to Our Lady, the Virgin Mary, and hadn't she got herself pregnant from another source whilst betrothed to Joseph? In any case, what would Father David do for a living if he left the church ministry? He explained that, since he was a trained accountant, this would present no proble. However, he indicated that he would stay on provided Liz would agree to a church wedding. Although, from what Faith and Charity told him, he supposed he could get away with just sleeping with her, he preferred to follow the tenets of his faith in this respect as in all things.

Faith and Charity were greatly relieved. 'And if it's all right with you, we'll ask Parson Thurlow to come out from retirement to tie the knot,' they chorused.

'And who better?' Father David chuckled.

By this time Roy's and Verity's son Martin, having trained as a teacher and gained a degree in mathematics, was teaching at a school in Somerset. Being able to remain in the village throughout one's life was the exception rather than the rule, which meant that his parents accepted both his success and his departure with equanimity. With Moira it was different. Not having the academic abilities of either her brother or sister, she had of necessity to make do with less mentally demanding work. Fortunately, a vacancy having arisen at Ashden Hall Gardens, she soon found a job working there as a trainee gardener under Roy's guidance. Having suffered as much as anyone over Dan's sad loss, she prospered from working with her number two father figure, her natural father Roy.

Despite the influence Sisterhood had in village affairs, most Ashden residents continued to behave in conventional fashion - at least outwardly. What wasn't so apparent to any outside observer was the ascendancy of its womenfolk, and this mainly because they achieved their purpose without ostentation. Men often appeared to be in charge when, in fact, they were little more than ciphers or fronts for the female brains behind the scenes. The Sisterhood had no problem with men both appearing big and talking big as long as they were not actually guiding the ship. Furthermore, as far as they were concerned, **apparent** moral values were no more than a cover for **real** moral values. As far as they were concerned, successful family life wasn't ensured because of any marriage bond imposed by an extraneous body, but through happy human relationships. Furthermore, what was right for some, didn't always work for others. Although for many, straightforward husband-wife-father-mother-children relationships worked well, for many others they did not. It was always more important **how** we did something than **what** we did or **why** we did it. Melanie, Jane and Liz in Bumber Close had chosen a certain method that seemed to be working out well. Other folk were in conventional marriages that were not proving successful. In other circumstances, the opposite of this scenario might well be the case. The main thing was to find a method that suited the participants and then make it work to the benefit of all concerned. Easier said than done, of course; but that was no reason for sticking to customs revealed, by an honest appraisal of history, to have caused untold suffering down the ages. For the Sisterhood, there was no such thing as moral absolutes, but simply moral values. Absolutes were always illusions simply because polarities were always related to each other. In other words, love and hate, good and bad, life and death, were no more and no less than opposite poles of the same entities. It's good to hate bad things and bad to love bad things. We can have too much of a good thing and the sensing of something bad warns us not to touch or eat it. Without death life would not be possible and vice versa. What is bad to day could be good tomorrow and vice -versa. Reasoning this way, the Sisterhood believed that hard and fast rules never helped anyone. To have Mother as Master and Father as Friend was always the best recipe for a happy and successful society; and in Ashden, Mother meant Master.

Over the years, Bumber Close had become a haven for wildlife. Hedgehogs visited the gardens, where some of them bred and had babies and the ring of mixed hedgerows surrounding the whole area attracted a wide variety of bird species. During the summer months house martins built their mud nests under the eves of the cottages and swallows built theirs on the rafters of sheds. The current Lord Denver had continued the policy of managing the estate as much as possible to help and encourage wildlife, a policy facilitated by the careful management of large areas of park and woodland. A shrewd man, Lord Denver was well aware of what was going on under his nose in his demesne. However, since he could see that it was helping life run more smoothly for everyone, he was more than happy to foster its continuance after a clandestine fashion.

The wedding took place the following June and, after a ten day honeymoon, David and Liz returned to live at the rectory - that's to say, ostensibly, for Liz both kept her cottage on in

Bumber Close and continued with her current research work at UCL. Since, having agreed to marry Father David, Liz had proceeded to seduce him right away, it was lucky for him that their shenanigans hadn't resulted in her becoming pregnant. Since Liz loved him to bits, if such a thing had happened, she would have seen him to rights. Inexperienced with women and shy with her at first, his technique soon improved under her tutelage. Nevertheless, none of this prevented her wearing him out during the honeymoon, during which she eventually found herself with child for the second time.

On their wedding night, Liz had divulged the identity of Jeremy's father. David was relieved. In the few years he had been Rector of Ashden he had grown to hold Roy in high esteem. Liz had decided to leave Jeremy under the care of his nanny in Bumber Close. Having grown fond of both Roy and Verity, he spent many happy hours playing in their garden, where Roy rigged things up for him and taught him all kinds of useful little skills. Reciprocating for Roy's help with Jane, Verity treated the little boy as if he were one of her own. Unaware of his relationship to either of them, he called them both by their forenames. Roy had no problem with that: fatherhood was a state of being, not something in a neatly labelled box tied up with ribbons.

By this time, Jane had given birth to Oscar, sired on her by Roland, who had arranged to have money invested for the child besides contributing towards his upkeep on a regular basis. For her part, Jane was anxious that the boy wouldn't grow up with an inflated idea of his own importance as a consequence of knowing who he father was. For this reason, she had contemplated leaving the village, but eventually decided against it after consulting with other members of the

Sisterhood. So a second Nanny called Rita was hired to live in with Susan and care for the little ones in Bumber Close, thus allowing Jane to return to her duties as estate manager at Ashden Hall where Hazel Trotter, her second in command, had been skilfully holding the fort during her confinement.

So it was that, as the years passed, the children of Bumber Close began attending at Ashden village school. Time wore on into the nineteen eighties, the Falklands War came and went, Roy was in his fifties and Mary, Faith and Charity had all climbed well into their seventies. The Sisterhood continued to flourish and all seemed set fair for a happy future for the village. Then came the storm that was to change everything.

Chapter 13

Storm

It was the night of 16 October 1987 and Nanny Susan was sleeping with Ted Mouser in his big bed at Elm Farm, Teddlethwaite. Tired of living alone and having given up on Melanie ever agreeing to marry him, Ted had turned his attention to Susan, who was only too pleased to accept his offer of marriage. Caring for other people's children had increased her natural desire to become a mother. So it was that she had fallen into the habit of spending her nights off with Ted. Melanie was relieved. Not being the marrying type, she was only too pleased that Susan had relieved her from that pressure. With any luck, she and Ted would have a couple of kids. Ted liked children; he was good with Jeremy; but Melanie really didn't want any more. It would, of course, mean losing a good nanny, but Rita, the other nanny, was already proving her worth and, anyway, another nanny could be found to replace Susan.

Ted was a good, kind man and Susan liked being with him. Her view was that, for a man-woman relationship to last, the participants needed to be friends as well as lovers. Passion was no substitute for mutual understanding, which was something that certainly existed between her and Ted. She also loved little Jeremy because he was Ted's and, if the need ever arose, she knew she would be able to count him as one of theirs. She had also grown very fond of the eccentric Melanie, not least because she was such a fascinating individualist with all kinds of inspiring ideas. Although Susan had no problem with Ted continuing to bed Melanie from time to time, such a scenario seemed increasingly unlikely, mainly because Melanie gave all the appearances of having turned her attention elsewhere.

Ted and Susan had their wedding day planned for the following May. Although Ted had no compunctions about shagging Susan before wedlock, he was anxious that she did not become pregnant until after they were wed. Although he would not have admitted it even to himself, Susan was sure this was on account of what had happened with Melanie who, having had Jeremy by him, then refused to wed him. However, she had preferred to take every precaution not to conceive rather than trying to reassure him that she would not renege on getting married no matter what happened. Although Ted certainly enjoyed 'getting his oats', he was equally happy just to cuddle up to her, a feeling that she very much reciprocated.

It was during one such pre-sleep cuddle on that particular night that Ted suddenly relinquished his hold and sat up the bed remarking on how wild the wind sounded. Sitting up beside him, Susan agreed. 'You can almost feel the house move,' she said.

Getting out of bed, Ted went to look out of the window. 'My God!' he exclaimed. 'They'll be trees down and tiles off at this rate.'

Slipping out of bed to join him, Susan watched in amazement as the wind tore at the branches of a great oak standing in the home paddock not far from the farm buildings.

Seconds later, an extra strong gust tore at the ancient tree, ripping it up by the roots to crash with an almighty roar, its branches smashing into the roof of the nearest building. Susan clung to Ted and he hugged her back. He felt like crying. It was as if he had just lost a very dear friend. Sadly, the great oak wasn't the only dear friend to meet its end that night.

Several hours earlier, Faith was driving home from a Sisterhood committee meeting at Lisa's Lodge when another mighty oak had crashed onto her car near the Green Man, crushing her to death. Venturing out from the near empty pub, its landlord was the first person to encounter the aftermath of the crash. He called first the police and then the ambulance, but neither were sure they could get there. Trees were falling and blocking roads everywhere. In any case, they told him, if, as he said, the tree had crushed the car flat, no one in it could possibly have survived. His two remaining customers returned with him to the scene of the tragedy, but there was nothing the three of them could do. It would require a crane of some kind to lift the heavy trunk from the car. So, not knowing what else to do, they decided to seek help from the village. On the way, they met up with Roy and two other men battling along into the wind to find out what had happened. Realising that it might well be Faith returning home around that time, he was anxious for her safety. Then, as the five men returned to the scene of the crash, his worst fears were realised when, kneeling down and peering under the mighty tree trunk, he focussed his hand torch and read the number plate.

It was dawn before sawing up the tree and clearing it could begin and near mid day before Faith's body was removed. Numbed by the shock, Roy moved around as if in a dream. Verity drove over to fetch Charity round to Bumber Close, where Roy's mother Mary did her best to comfort her in her distress. Father David came to see them and a great sadness descended on the whole village. Faith had been more than well liked: she was loved and respected by everyone, and this because of her blatant sexuality rather than in spite of it. Since the way she did things always helped rather than hindered, her contribution to village life had been highly valued. Her long association with the late Lord Denver had brought her status rather than condemnation, and the church authorities had always chosen to overlook any so called 'shortcomings' in such an accomplished musician. She had been a vibrant example of the triumph of goodness over morality: that's to say, **supposed** morality, for her way of doing things were ultimately of higher ethical standard than that of the defective moral code she had ostensibly flouted. None knew this better than Parson Thurlow and his good wife Flora.

The passing of time did nothing to assuage Roy's grief. Now that he had lost her, he realised for the first time that Faith had been the love of his life. There was so much that he shared with her, not least their mutual love of music. More than that, she had initiated him into the rites of lovemaking with a compassionate understanding not enjoyed by most men.She was a teacher par excellence in everything she did. Fated not to bear children, she was a caring mother to all with whom she had contact, not least to the many children she had taught at Teddlethwaite school. Regarding men as overgrown children, she had guided their sexuality as if she were teaching them to read and write. This had been particularly true of the old Lord Denver, Roy and Parson Thurlow, none of whom had realised their full sexual potential until she had schooled them in the arts of lovemaking. Indeed, for Faith, living every moment of every day had been an art. For her, the highest moral standards were achieved as one might paint a picture, write a poem or compose a piece of music. If beauty was in the eye of the beholder, then morals were measures rather than absolutes, and hers had been a made to measure world in which one size never fitted all.

Saint Mary's Parish Church wasn't large enough to hold all those who attended Faith's funeral service that was jointly conducted by Father David and Parson Thurlow, and during which Roy was given an opportunity to pay tribute to his dear friend. Verity understood perfectly. Knowing what it was to love two men, she could appreciate his love for two women. Now, with Dan and Faith both gone, there was just the two of them. They were fortunate to have each other. Charity was denied that luxury. Like Roy, Verity realised that love came in many different forms. The way she had, and still, loved Dan was not the same as she loved Roy - similar maybe, but not the same - and this was also true of Roy's love for more than one woman. Just as Faith was the love of Roy's life, Dan was the love of hers. However, this didn't mean that she and Roy were any the less in love with each other for all that. True love was born of understanding, and those who truly loved each other would understand all other loves in each of their lives. This is why she had been able to loan Roy to Liz. Had she not done so, Liz might well not now be happily married to Father David.

As the months passed Roy gradually came to terms with his sad loss. Working in Ashden Hall Gardens had helped as also had going for walks in the park, where he could get away from all human contact and relate to the living wilderness around him. As winter drew to a close, all kinds of birds began to pair up and build, re-build or repair their nests ready for mating and hatching, and he found solace in the cawing of rooks in the great rookery in the tall trees near the churchyard where it joined onto the deer park. Green woodpeckers flew low, fluting forth their yaffling calls, as they undulated over the anthills, and he was equally delighted with the 'tueeh-tueeh' piping call of a nuthatch that was nesting again with its mate in a hole it had reduced in size by plastering it round with mud in the branch of a tall ash tree. He also knew where a pair of little owls had decided to nest at ground level in an old hollow tree stump. Faith's life had been of the same vibrant quality as that exhibited by these wild creatures, who cared about building their nests and rearing their young just as she had cared about Ashden and all that went on in it.

It was on an evening in late April, about an hour before dusk, when Roy had meandered into the park in meditative mood to savour the scents and sounds of spring in the still air, that he came across Melanie seated on the dipping branch of an old, gnarled tree, one of a whole grove of hawthorns. Swinging gently to and fro, she was humming away to herself, but not so preoccupied as to fail to notice his approach. On catching sight of her, he hesitated as if about to turn and walk away, but she called to him and he had little choice but to make his way over to her. Although they were neighbours, they had never related to each other to any great extent apart form the usual social contacts.

Melanie patted the branch beside her. 'Come! Sit yourself down and share your thoughts with me.'

Taken aback by such an invitation from someone he didn't know very well, Roy hesitated, but Melanie's bright smile overcame his misgivings and he soon found himself seated shoulder to shoulder and thigh to thigh beside her in the limited space available. She was wearing a green cardigan over a green and yellow patterned, calf-length dress. Although blue would have matched best with her bright eyes, her chosen colours seemed more appropriate in the burgeoning green of the hawthorn grove. Her flowing fair hair certainly fitted in with the sense of renewal in everything around her, and Roy was aware of a delicate, indeterminate perfume emanating from no particular source, it being an all pervading wonderment of woman and wilderness. They must have sat thus for several minutes as if each were waiting for the other to speak first, before Melanie was the first to speak in a conciliatory tone of voice as if she were attempting to reassure some nervous child.

'There really isn't anything for you to be afraid of, you know.'

'You think I'm afraid?'

'Yes, I do. First you tried to avoid me and then you were in two minds about sitting next to me. Is that not so?'

'I can't deny it.'

'Well, that's something: it means you're honest with yourself and, that being so, it'll be no big step for you to admit that you would've preferred to have found Faith here; is that not so?'

Roy nodded. 'It's the way she went - so sudden, so unexpected. If she'd died of old age, then they'd have been time to say goodbye, if you see what I mean. Now, I keep thinking about all the things I wanted to tell her and didn't.'

Melanie reached round the back of him with her right arm. 'Well, now you can tell me. I've been appointed Priestess to the Sisterhood in her place.'

'Priestess to the Sisterhood?' Roy echoed in a bewildered tone of voice.

'Yes, that's right. There's much you don't know about us. The truth is, you didn't need to then. Faith had made it plain that you were her chosen one, her consort, and we all accepted that; but now they've chosen me and, since there needs to be continuity, we'd all prefer it if you'd agree to be my consort. It's all to do with continuity - tying in with what's gone before - if you see what I mean.'

Roy was desolate. Why could Faith not have told him everything? 'I didn't… I didn't know this,' he faltered.

'You mustn't blame Faith. She interpreted the rules as she thought best. You also need to realise that, if it hadn't been for her, you wouldn't have been taken into our confidence as much as you have been. Be that as it may, I know how much she valued you and, following on from that, I've decided to allow you to become involved with us a step further - in memory of her and, more than that, because I know it's what she would've wanted for you.' As Melanie was speaking, the pressure form her arm increased as if to emphasise her concern.

Reassured by Melanie's explanation, Roy asked about the 'extra step'. She did her best to explain. As he already knew, the Sisterhood was a society of women set up to foster the re-establishment of female primacy in all aspects of human society. Although it wasn't a religious organisation, it had adopted some quasi-religious rituals as a way to foster bonding and a sense of belonging among the membership. Amongst other things, this involved the creation of the office of priestess, a valued member elected to preside over the meetings and ceremonies of the society. The term *Priestess* had been preferred to that of *president* in order to honour the memory of those matriarchal cultures that had existed in many places prior to the advent of the so called *Heroic Age*. Since the Sisterhood had been Faith's brain child, who better to be its first priestess? Melanie had recently been elected to take her place. Since most members lived far away and could attend only a few meetings during the course of a year, it was thought best to have a priestess who lived reasonably near Lisa's Lodge. Melanie with her strong personality and pleasant manner had been an obvious choice, or so Roy guessed, modesty having prevented her from suggesting anything of that kind.

Melanie went on to discuss the relationship between life forms and landscape. In order to survive, all living things needed to be able both to find food and blend in with their chosen landscape. When we lose our sense of belonging to the landscape, we set ourselves on a path leading to the eventual annihilation of our species. Harmony with the landscape fosters serenity within our selves and with others. This leads to respect for each other, teaching us never to enter into any kind of relationship without regard for the needs of any other person or persons involved. Taking hold of Roy's right hand, Melanie placed it over her left breast beneath the flimsiness of her flowered frock. Although surprised by the action Roy did not resist, savouring instead the neat firmness of the hillock within the cup of his hand as she continued her discourse. Just as the landscape was shaped into downs, dales, caves, clefts and so on, so was the body, which was to be cherished and respected just as one would respect a beautiful landscape.

Sadly, just as landscapes are often raped and ruined by the hand of man, so are women's bodies. Roy was the epitome of the kind of man the Sisterhood wished to foster. He had been selected by Faith the Priestess to be trained into becoming the kind of man who would respect the landscape of womankind. Sexual relations should always be how, when and where the woman wanted them to be, and not there just for the slaking of the lust of randy males. It was for the woman to choose her mate or mates and for her to decide when and where she would mate and how many children she would bear. Sadly, women were now cursed with monthly periods. When humans were still hunter gatherers, moving from place to place, it is most likely that oestrus occurred just once a year. Easier living in settled conditions with a good food supply caused an increase in fertility.

Roy understood well what Melanie was explaining to him. He had coupled with Faith, Verity and Liz because each one of them had wanted him to do just that and not because he had pressed any one of them to give into his desires. Now he had a distinct feeling that Melanie was about to ask him to oblige her in similar fashion. He hadn't long to wait. There was to be a coupling, but not here and now. It was planned for May Day at a special ceremony. In vain did Roy protest that, at fifty eight, he was passed that kind of thing. The solemnity of the ritual demanded experienced and steady participants. Verity had already been consulted and had no objections to Roy being used in this capacity. Indeed, the Sisterhood was at one in believing the suggested rite to be a fitting memorial to the memory of Faith, now regarded as their founding mother - and who better to perform it in her memory than her protégé Roy and her successor Melanie?

With a sigh of resignation, Roy placed his right arm round Melanie's waist and turned his head to nose into the inviting flow of her hair, murmuring as he did so: 'So be it... For Faith's sake, I can't refuse. In any case, you're now what she was: tall, fair and fondling - like the landscape of this village, my mother Ashden, that I love so much.'

Chapter 14

Bonobo

All thirteen of the local membership of the Sisterhood, along with four national members, were present for the May Day celebrations at Lisa's Lodge, which on this occasion had been combined with Melanie's inauguration as Priestess with Roy as her chosen consort. The rite, consisting of a colourful combination of chanting, singing and dancing, was in the way of being a celebration of the fertility of Mother Earth, fostering respect for the fragility of emerging life within the context of motherhood as protector against pollution. Although, ideally, the ritual would have been best performed entirely outside at dawn, it had been moved to the evening to fit in with the working and domestic commitments of members, with much of it being performed inside in the assembly hall to avoid disturbing wildlife with undue noise and movement. However, it did begin outside with a colourful procession through the gardens and round the flower meadow, after which the participants processed into the assembly hall for the main part of the proceedings.

Through his long involvement with the Sisterhood, Roy was familiar with many of the songs, chants and customs. He had long since become the leading male among the three or four men they called upon whenever they felt the need for a male presence in any of their rituals which, it has to be said, were neither frequent nor over-played. The Sisterhood was a society for the fostering of the development of a matriarchal society, not an excuse for participation in mumbo-jumbo witchery. It wasn't that there was any prejudice against witches as such; members simply had other priorities. This being so, the members had no problem with adapting their ceremonies to suit any particular occasion. Since Faith had been the number one founder member of the Sisterhood, she had simply 'grown', as it were, into being recognised as its Priestess, which meant that Melanie's was their first ever priestess inauguration ceremony.

Believing the fostering of a delicate natural balance to be the best way of achieving harmony in the world, the Sisterhood were keen to encourage responsible attitudes towards procreation and parentage. The necessity not to have large families in an already overcrowded world meant that sexuality had to be channelled into other avenues of creativity, not least of which was the belief that coupling between the sexes could be developed into a fulfilling art form as an end in itself. In such a scenario the woman must always be in control, becoming pregnant only when it was her desire to do so. It must always be the woman who chooses the man and not the other way round. Women were neither a horde of glorified whores for the satisfaction of male lust nor mere baby machines fulfilling a male-devised view of sexual morality. Men were there to satisfy female needs if and when they occurred. In return, sensible women would always devise ways of satisfying bona fide male needs, but always through carefully controlled methods such as any good mother might use when disciplining her children. Rocking horse rides should never be confused with mounting a mare to produce a foal. There was a time and place for each of these acts and one of them was no less important than the other.

Clad diaphanously in flowing robes, the Sisterhood danced, weaving to and fro and in and out amongst each other in the assembly hall at Lisa's Lodge in time to music provided, in the main, by fiddle, drum and accordion. Dressed in green and yellow, her flowing hair ringed with a floral coronet, Melanie took the lead with Roy, the only male present, as her consort clad in loose white shirt and olive green trousers. A natural dancer, Roy readily adapted himself in both style and rhythm to every nuance of the elaborate ritual. Having been trained by Faith to fit in with feminine dominance, he was content to comply with it outwardly whilst, at the same time, inwardly exalting in his liberation from the coils of convention. Since the Sisterhood had given him the stage on which to flaunt his dislike of macho male culture, there was no way he could deny them his aid in anything they might set out to achieve. Gardening, walking, running, dancing and a healthy diet had kept him slim and supple beyond his years.

Presently, curtains at the far end of the assembly hall were drawn back to reveal an alcove lavishly decorated with flowers and containing a broad, bouncy-looking couch. Then, as the dancers whirled around the room and Roy and Melanie reached the entrance to this ante-chamber, she suddenly led him, leaping onto the couch and twirling round causing her abundant hair to flare around her in wild abandon as she proceeded to disrobe in flaunting fashion. Leaving go her hands, Roy stood and gasped at the fascination of it all. Here was something special. Used as he was both to indulging beautiful women and to enjoying their favours, he had never before experienced anything like this. If Faith had been his comforting, motherly mentor of mutual delights, Verity his loving wife and devoted mother of their children and Liz the imp who had seduced him in a cheeky act of defiance, then Melanie was the Queen of Heaven. The swirl of her hair above the bounce of her breasts and buttocks, along with the inviting quiver of her thighs and muscular modulations of her belly muscles, were an inspiration, and an irresistible one at that. In such a scenario, preventing her from disrobing him was out of the question, as Melanie knew only too well as she reached out to divest him of his shirt and trousers in the exaggerated fashion demanded by the musical tempo.

Coupling with such a woman was all part of the dance routine that went on around the two of them as they set about performing the game of love. Neither of them doubted that they were acting out the Rite of Spring, symbolising the renewal of the life force, the essence of understanding and without which nothing was knowable. As Melanie received Roy into her, she knew it was as if the offspring of the womb were seeking to return home to its eternal mother without whom there could be no real harmony. For Roy it was as if he were melting into the bliss of eternal childhood; for had they not all played with him as if he were their child - a child who would give them yet more children, or not as the case may be? So what now? He wanted no more fatherhood; but it wasn't for him to decide. He must do as Melanie wanted and only she could decide such things.

The coupling completed and the Rite of Spring performed, the assembled members re-robed the couplers and bore them in triumph to enthrone them together as King and Queen of the May. As Faith's successor, Melanie had now also taken control of her chosen consort in the shape of Roy. However, it was to be a symbolic takeover; Melanie would not expect Roy to perform with her as he had done with Faith; she has simply felt the need to have him this once as a tribute to her much loved and respected predecessor in the office of Priestess to the Sisterhood. Realising that it would be unfair to impose more fatherhood on him, she had made sure that she would not become pregnant; but not without some misgivings. She wouldn't have minded having another child, and especially by one as decent as Roy, but she had to be realistic. Since she wasn't keen to take on a permanent husband, just the one child, her daughter Carol, would be as much as she'd want to cope with in the way of offspring.

By this time, Roy's daughter Moira had become well established as a gardener at Ashden Hall; so much so, in fact, that there was every reason to suppose that she would take over from him as head gardener when he eventually retired. A shy girl and under-achiever at school, she had found her vocation with plants and was soon expert at almost anything to do with them and their needs as she backed up her practical skills with avid reading and study concerning anything to do with both botany and gardening. One of the results of such commitment was that she had preserved specimens of virtually all the flora in and around Ashden along with careful notes concerning the plants individual requirements, prevalence, endangerment and so on. In the process she had been careful to note the prevalence of pollinating insects as well as identifying likely pests and their predators. Understandably proud of her, Roy had long since felt able to tell her about her true parentage. Having been fond of her step-father Dan, she found solace in her love and respect for the second father figure in her life. Wrapped in her own interests, Moira had little time for either boy friends or in joining the Sisterhood, of which she knew little. Fortunately for her, her horticultural capabilities were so effective that the other gardeners employed at Ashden Hall had little choice but to defer to her in every respect, thus making it easier for her to assume a firm authoritative stance that augured well for when she would eventually take over from Roy as head gardener.

As the nineteen eighties drew to a close and Roy passed his sixtieth birthday, he felt closer to Verity than ever before and she to him. Verity was convinced that the underlying cause for failure in human relationships was a lack of appreciation of each others needs. She had no time for those who indulged in ***one size fits all*** moral standards. As she saw it, for some folk, when morality entered the door, compassion flew out of the window. Since she and Roy had sorted out both their love life and their family affairs in a way that worked well for them and theirs, she failed to see how more conventional moral standards could be regarded as being superior to their own home grown behavioural code. As 1990 approached, the only cloud on her horizon emerged in the shape of Emma on the latter's return from studying the family life of bonobo chimps in the Congo.

Emma, now in her late fifties, lost no time in renewing contact with her old friend Roy who, although pleased to see her, felt ill at ease with someone he supposed to be without any real love life, and this more especially so on account of this being the underlying reason for Verity's dislike of her. Whilst quite prepared to loan her husband out for bona fide relationships concerned with the affairs of the Sisterhood, she resented Emma for having ventured, in the past, to commandeer Roy's mind for her own specific research; or so it seemed to her. In other words, Verity saw Emma as a woman who contrived to wear drawers and a red hat at the same time, and this was simply not playing an honest game. However, as Roy soon realised, Emma had changed, and it was all due to the bonobos.

Unlike common chimpanzee society, which was male led, bonobo society was dominated by senior females with each group always being led by a matriarch. Bonobos had also developed sexual relations beyond their procreative purpose to include a bonding process, containing comforting techniques applicable to a wide variety of needs. Since this system worked well for our closely living animal relatives, Emma saw no reason why it should not work well for humans, especially seeing as bonobo society was considerably less aggressive and violent than that of the common chimps. Her research had also led her to believe that many human societies of four or five thousand years ago had been matriarchal and much less cruel than became the case after the advent of the so called 'Heroic Age' that heralded the beginning of the prevalence of male dominated societies throughout the world. Sadly, in the present state of world affairs, even when women found themselves in positions of power, they were forced to fit in with Heroic Age values in order to maintain any kind of firm control over both national and international affairs. Margaret Thatcher was a case in point. Having deemed it necessary to out-man the men in order to retain power, she had finally over-stepped the mark by introducing the manifestly unfair poll tax, which was utterly detested by the conservative minded inhabitants of Ashden and its surrounding villages. As far as Emma was concerned, here was a woman who had betrayed the fair bonobo principles of matriarchal government in favour of chauvinistic male dominance.

Since it was a long established custom on the Ashden Estate for its main employees to be allowed to live rent and rates free in its cottages even after retirement, Lord Denver was horrified by the poll tax, which the estate could not afford to pay as it had done the rates. Brought up in the One Nation Tory tradition, he was glad when the Iron Lady was forced to resign and the poll tax replaced by something at least a little fairer. One could only assume that Mrs Thatcher had never heard of bonobos or, if she had, she thoroughly disapproved of their methods.

Emma was intrigued by the setup in Bumber Close, which she saw as being run in a very bonobo-like fashion. In particular, she was delighted with Melanie, seeing her as a worthy successor to Faith, for whom she'd always had great respect. She saw the children as being well disciplined in the care of strong and dedicated women backed up by Roy and one or two other reliable father figures such as the Honourable Roland and Ted Mouser. Whereas Roland was now beneficially wed to an affluent member of the aristocracy, who had since provided him with an heir, the latter was happily wed to Susan, the erstwhile nanny, who was now the proud mother of two thriving boys. Still very fond of Ted, Melanie was always welcoming whenever he came to see Carol, his daughter by her, who would sometimes return with him to stay overnight at Elm Farm, Teddlethwaite, where Susan was happy for her to spend some time with her little half-brothers. As for Roland and Jane, things were not so good there. He doted on Oscar and wanted to continue his relationship with Jane, but she would have none of it, insisting that such a liaison would not fit in with her position as estate manager, which she was determined to keep. Like Melanie, she had little interest in marriage, preferring instead to indulge a steady paramour, a shy wee farmer from Felsham called Coy, whom it pleased her to pleasure if only to make him feel wanted in the midst of the trials and tribulations of trying to make ends meet on his two hundred acres of arable land. Oscar had grown very fond of Coy, preferring him to his own father, whom he saw as not truly belonging in the same world he shared with the agile little farmer. Liking it that way, Jane continued to encourage Coy's interest, going out with him sometimes and occasionally allowing him to bounce around and pleasure himself on her obvious attractions, enjoying herself equally in the process. All this being so, Roland had little choice but to accept things as they were and get on with life.

By this time Roy had taken to spending more time dropping in to see his mother Mary, now well into her eighties and increasingly fragile. He had long realised that it was she he had to thank for his long friendship with Faith and Charity. It was as if Mary had deliberately arranged for him to be seduced by them, thus ensuring that he would become imbedded within a magical world from which there was no escape. Never herself a member of the Sisterhood, she was nevertheless in sympathy with its aims, and was thus in favour of Roy's association with it. Much loved and respected by all who lived in Bumber Close and beyond, everyone felt a great loss when Roy found her dead in her arm chair by the fire when he called in to see her one frosty January day early in 1990. A few weeks later, Charity joined her in Saint Mary's churchyard. In many ways, it was the end of an era. Nevertheless, Roy was determined that the new one would retain much of what had been good about the old one. In varying ways, Verity, Jane, Emma, Melanie and Moira were all very supportive of him, and he was grateful for that. By the summer of that year, Emma had bought Kiln House form the estate as her retirement home and was soon very much part of village life. Soon becoming good friends, she and Melanie worked tirelessly together to promote the aims of the Sisterhood, but it was uphill work in an increasingly frenetic world. Mary's cottage was let to an estate employee and his family, all of whom soon fitted in well with life in Bumber Close.

Roy had formed the habit of bringing flowers from the hall gardens to place on the graves of the three women, Faith, Charity and Mary, who had been such an influence in his life, and it was on one such occasion that he met up with his long since retired half-brother Fred. Since they'd never related well to each other, it was no surprise that they hadn't seen each other for some time. Having run on about his son and how well he was doing in the family building business that had grown out of the old wheelwright's yard, he presently adopted a wistful tone as he remarked how fortunate Roy had been. Since Roy had always gained the impression that Fred had looked down on him as a mere gardener, he was somewhat surprised to hear this and, in keeping with his forthright character, lost no time in saying so.

Smiling wanly, Fred tried to explain. 'Well, it's like this: you're different; you've… Well, you've escaped the rat race.'

Roy's eyebrows shot up. 'You mean, you haven't?'

Fred nodded. 'Hmm… That's right. Most of us haven't. Success is like that - if you can call it success.'

'What else should you call it?' Roy said brightly, trying to strike a positive note. 'And all credit due to you, I say. You should be a happy man.'

'Happy man?' Fred echoed. 'Well, yes, I suppose so; but

what **is** happiness? I suppose, in their own way, rats are happy in a sewer. As I see it, theirs happiness and theirs happiness: the sort you work for, and the sort that just sort of comes out - emerges - if you get my meaning.'

Roy thought he did. 'You mean, it's sort of like happiness that you put on and happiness that comes from the inside?'

Fred nodded. 'That's right. At least, it's something like that. Look... You and me... We've never really got on - like each other - that kind of thing. Fact is, we live in different worlds. I'm suited to mine and I've done well, and I can't honestly say that I'd like to have done things any differently; but that doesn't stop me... stop me..'

'Stop you doing what?'

'Stop me doing nothing. What I mean is... Well, it doesn't stop me envying you, a man at peace with himself.'

'And you're not? At peace with yourself, I mean.'

Looking at the ground, Fred slowly shook his head. 'You can see for yourself. I mean, who is these days. Unless yourself, and there aren't many around like you.'

Tears in his eyes, Roy looked away. Only too well did he know that, even in the midst of sorrow, he had never ceased to be happy. How could he ever be anything else when Mary, Faith and Charity had always wanted it that way for him? The way of happiness was the way of the womb, the woman's way, and men were happy when they allowed themselves to be governed by it. Misery came when they insisted on regarding women as chattels, objects of desire and bearers of male heirs. Merely pretending not to do so was no good. Woman had sole control of Womb, and the universe was the Great Womb. Men could either learn to live peacefully within it or destroy life on earth by continuing to follow their own selfish, anti-womb agenda of strife and destruction.

It was just as Roy reached out with his hand to shake Fred's that Moira came running into the churchyard calling out to them: 'Come! Come quickly! There's been an accident! It's Roland! He's been thrown from his horse!'

Chapter 15

Rita

The Honourable Roland, paralysed from the waist down as a result of his accident, never fully recovered and was dead by the turn of the century, leaving his, by then, legitimate teenage son Rupert as heir to both the estate and the title. Consequent upon the accident, his wife, the Honourable Louise, came to know the details of Oscar's parentage. Fortunately for Jane, far from turning against her, Louise took her into her confidence as a special friend who would understand her predicament. Indeed, as time passed, she soon came to realise that such a friend outside of her class and social round was a real friend indeed. Jane became the one confidant she knew she could trust absolutely. So it came about that, for her part, Jane continued to prosper as estate manager and her sister, Moira, for hers, continued set fair to become head gardener, all much to Roy's satisfaction. His only anxiety was that the current Lord Denver would survive long enough to see his grandson, the young Rupert, well passed his minority with some experience behind him. But this is all to forge too far ahead too soon. Before the time came round for Roland to pass on, Roy was to have one last adventure that was to endear him in the memory of the Sisterhood beyond anything he could have imagined, and it all began with Rita, the nanny who had taken over in Bumber Close after Susan's marriage to Ted Mouser.

As Carol, Oscar, Jeremy and her other charges grew older and started school, Rita gradually became a housekeeper rather than a nanny. Now nearly thirty five, she had become so used to caring for other folk's children that she doubted if she would ever want to be bothered with any of her own - if 'bothered' was the right word. Since it was likely that her charges would all want to keep in touch her even after they were grown up with families of their own, she thought that this would be enough to cope with without having children of her own. A capable, self-sufficient person, she derived too much satisfaction from the everyday round for her to have any real desire to team up with a male partner. As for sexual relations, her view was that lasting contentment was always preferable to fleeting, conceptual thrills, anyone of which might lead into the realms of the unwanted. It was therefore of little surprise that she tended to be just a tiny bit over-weight, a condition that many a discerning male would have described as 'pleasantly plump'. A straight-haired brunette with brown eyes, she tended to wear her hair in a long pigtail that bounced around behind her as she worked and moved around. Concerned about her future after all her charges had left school, Verity discussed her with Roy, who thought that, with her experience, she would have no difficulty in finding more work as a nanny.

Verity frowned. 'But that's not the point. What you say is like selling her on after she's given us all such sterling service.'

Expressing his appreciation of that analysis, Roy added: 'But what else do you suggest?'

'Well, she's a good housekeeper. There's surely someone round here who needs one, or will do sooner or later. Then she could remain around here near her friends. It seem her parents are dead and she was an only child.'

'She could find herself a nice man and marry him.'

'Oh Roy, really! Don't be so silly! You know as well as anyone that you can't find a partner just like that.'

'Can't you? All I know is, you found me - just like that.'

Verity giggled and they said no more little realising that, with the passage of time, Rita's predicament would fine its own solution.

Some years passed and Father David was as lonely as he'd ever been. Immersed in her research work, Liz was spending less and less time in Ashden and their daughter Anne was away at boarding school. Although Father David had been against sending her there, Liz had insisted on it. Having enjoyed her time at a girls' boarding school, she saw no reason why Anne shouldn't have a similar experience. Father David would have liked at least one more child, hopefully a son, but Liz wouldn't hear of it, not least because it would have meant her having to endure a third pregnancy. Anyway, what about Jeremy, her son by Roy? Was he not son enough for them both? David knew better. Jeremy was so obviously Roy's son in both looks and leanings that there was no way he could warm towards the lad other than to like him well enough as he might like any good natured, well mannered youngster anywhere. Somewhat reassured by her passionate lovemaking whenever Liz was with him, he was nevertheless suspicious that she might be having affairs with other men during her long absences from Ashden. Worse still, he was sometimes doubtful that his love for her was as strong as it had been. Being a parish priest could be a lonely job and he sometimes felt the need of some reassurance.

When she was with him, Liz did her best, but her efforts were not helped by her almost total lack of sympathy for his beliefs, a state of affairs that caused him constant concern.

So it came about that, when Father David was returning home from a therapeutic walk round the village in the lingering sunlight of a long June day, he decided, on impulse, to call in at Foxhole Cottage, Liz's one time dwelling place. What he expected to find there, he had no idea; but what he did find was a lonely Rita wondering about her future. Surprised to see him, she nevertheless invited him in after a brief hesitation, if only because she felt sorry for him on account of his forlorn demeanour.

'Is there something you wished to see me about?' she asked nonchalantly as she signed for him to sit on a chair by the kitchen table. 'We could go into the front room, only I brought you in here as I was in the middle of making myself a mug of barley cup. Would you like some? Or would you prefer coffee?'

'Barley cup will do just fine, and I don't mind the kitchen…' Hesitating, he looked at the floor.

Rita stirred the hot drinks. 'You've been out for a walk?'

Father David nodded. 'That's right. It's such a nice evening and…'

'And you thought you'd get out and enjoy it? I don't blame you. There! Here's your drink. I hope I haven't made it too sweet. I should have asked if you take sugar.' Taking up her own drink, Rita sat down at the opposite end of the table.

'Well, I do in these kind of drinks. Thanks! Look… It's

so kind of you to invite me in. I hadn't intended to make any calls. Only, you see… Well, Anne - that's my daughter - her mother, she kept this place on and, well, Ann lived here a lot as well as in the rectory and you were her nanny…' Father David hesitated.

Rita beamed him a reassuring smile. 'Well, part of the time I was. There was Susan too of course.'

'Ah yes! She's the one who married Ted Mouser; but it's you I know best.'

Although Rita nodded in polite agreement, she was inwardly unconvinced that he really knew her at all. It was more like as if he'd always taken her for granted. Suddenly she said: 'I'm not sure I'll be here much longer. As I'm sure you know, Liz - Mrs Doddington - is keeping this place on for the time being and I'm staying on as housekeeper. That's to say, until I find another position as nanny somewhere.'

Father David shifted uneasily. Since he knew nothing of any of this, he was at some loss to know how to respond, causing him to seek refuge in a non-committal: 'I see.'

Turning her head to glance sharply over table and straight at him, Rita said suddenly. 'No you don't! You don't see at all, do you?'

Father David looked at the floor as he retorted glumly: 'No, I'm afraid I don't.'

Feeling suddenly sorry for this decent, dedicated priest, Rita apologised. 'I'm sorry; I shouldn't have been so blunt. But the fact is… Well, I don't like to see anyone being made a fool of, least of all anyone as good as yourself.'

'Good? You think me good?'

'Well, yes I do. I know I'm not a religious person and don't attend church much - at least not now I've no children to look after - but that doesn't mean I don't appreciate all you do.'

'Well now, that's very kind of you. Anyway, I'd best be going. Thanks for the barley cup.' Father David stood up.

Throwing him a sharp look, Rita told him to sit down. 'You're going no where!' she said. A plan of action having suddenly formed in her mind, she watched with some satisfaction as the startled priest sank back meekly into his chair. Pressing home her advantage, she continued by asking him if he had always intended to marry one day, which of course he hadn't, and he was honest with her about that, even if he didn't feel able to go as far as admitting that Liz had seduced him into it.

Suddenly, Rita said: 'We're two of a kind!'

Father David's eyes widened. 'Two of a kind? I don't follow.'

Rita's thick, seductive tone of voice belied the directness of her response: 'We're neither of us the marrying kind.'

'You've never had a man friend? Never thought of marrying?' Father David sounded genuinely surprised.

Rita tried to explain. Like most girls she'd had boyfriends during her teens, but not since her first appointment after training as a nanny. It was if she'd skipped any falling in love and bearing children episodes in order to get down to serious mothering, which was something she enjoyed doing. Now that she was heading into her late thirties, it didn't seem to make any sense at all for her to marry and have children of her own. As for missing out on sex, well, she'd had a bit of that, but it was a poor substitute for looking after children. As far as she could see, all this talk about falling in love was little more than dressing up raw lust in fancy clothes. Yes, she had sometimes thought it would be nice to settle down in middle age with a good, kind man, but even good, kind men could be demanding and lustful. She'd be more interested in finding someone she could share interests with, but that was easier said than done. She wasn't interested in football, motor racing and that kind of thing like so many men seemed to be. What was the point of being wed to someone who always wanted to be 'out with the boys' in his spare time? As she saw it, there was far too little real love in the world. She resented being seen as a sex object. Women should be cared for and loved for what they were in themselves and not as mere sex objects for the slaking of male lust. No, she knew nothing about the Sisterhood. She wasn't one for joining organisations. Not that some didn't fulfil a useful purpose - no, it wasn't that, but simply that such bodies tended to become ends in themselves instead of influencing society as a whole. Maybe, had she been brighter at school, she could have played a greater role in the betterment of society. As it was, she fancied she might be doing a good job by influencing children for the better as they grew up.

Having listened intently to all that she had to say, Father David was impressed by her obvious sincerity, and he tried to tell her so without sounding too patronising. It wasn't easy. As he looked at her, taking in the honest rotundity of her kindly features, he found himself fumbling around for words until, cutting across his frustration with sudden determination, he exclaimed: 'Oh, damn it! What I really mean to say is: you're a hell of a lovely girl!'

'**Hell of a**, reverend? Tell me, is that better or worst than being heavenly?' Rita giggled as she looked straight at him and into his eyes.

Joining in with the laughter, Father David felt much better - and suddenly happier than he'd been for a long time. What a bloody fool he'd been to fall for a career driven workaholic academic such as Liz when he could have shared his vocation with a woman such as Rita who truly cared about people and who had such a deep appreciation of the needs of children. Then, looking straight at her, as he struggled to put his feeling into words, an inadvertent tear began to trickle down his care-worn cheek. Reaching for the kitchen roll, Rita tore off a section and came to the rescue. 'You're such a child, just one big child,' she murmured as she gently wiped his face.

Hitching up the skirt of her thin summer dress, Rota straddled Father David as he sat there on the kitchen chair and hugged him to her. Reciprocating by encircling her with his arms, he nosed her in the neck. Presently, leaning back a little, she looked longingly into his face. Lowering his gaze under the intensity of hers, he said suddenly: 'I can see right down between your tits.'

'Between my tits! What a thing for a man of the cloth to say!' Rita's tone of surprise was more affected than real.

Father David sighed. 'You have no idea what a strain it is having to act good all the time,' he said.

'Act good? And here's me thinking you were truly good!'

'Well, isn't being 'truly good', as you call it, all about being honest and calling a spade a spade? After all, even a priest needs to relax sometimes.'

Disentangling herself from his embrace, Rita stood up and held out a hand to him. 'Come! You're not going home tonight. You're a lost child, if ever there was one, and you're in need of some real mothering.'

Father David didn't resist. For the first time for a very long time he felt that he had come home. Leading him upstairs, she undressed him and put him to bed. Then, although she went on to strip off in front of him, there was no ensuing sexual act between them, but just an affectionate cuddling together as two wounded creatures might comfort each other after a frightening experience. Sleep soon followed with Rita the first to awake. Getting out of bed, she went over to the window to look out and savour the pristine delights of the dew drenched June dawn. Then, as Father David opened his eyes to glance straight into the delights presented by her sturdy thighs and well rounded buttocks, he experienced an overwhelming sense of belonging. As if aware of his appreciation of her, Rita turned to gaze down upon him as if she were admiring the qualities of one of her erstwhile charges. Then, as they exchanged smiles, she asked him if he'd slept well.

'Never better! And you?'

'Very well, thank you. That's to say, very well considering you're the first man I've ever slept with for a whole night. I've had it off with a boyfriend a few times in my youth, but I've never slept a whole night with any man.'

'Remarkable! And more remarkable still, you've now slept

a whole night with a man and haven't had it off with him.'

Getting back into bed, Rita pulled the duvet around her and sat up beside him. 'Tell me something: was Liz the first woman you ever did it with?'

'Hmm… Yes she was.'

'I thought so! And you thought you were in your seventh heaven?'

'Yes - something like that.'

Nodding thoughtfully for a few seconds, Rita presently said. 'That's the age old mistake so many couples make. What they fail to realise is that a successful relationship between a man and a woman is something like ninety nine percent mutual understanding and just one percent sexual compatibility. The problem is both love and sex are lotteries, and it's not always easy to tell the difference between them. To make matters worse, so called 'love at first sight' is just as likely to last as any other kind of love. It's not so difficult to know right away. The problem is how to know that the know that you know is the one that will last. There's always a risk. Be that as it may, I'll tell you this now: I've been offered a job as a day nanny with a working family over at Bobbington, the other side of Felsham, and I have to let them know by today if I'll take it. I was going to turn it down as I can't go on living here and I'd have nowhere else to live. But I've changed my mind. I'm going to tell them I'll take it because I'm going to come and live with you as your housekeeper.'

So it was that Rita went to live with Father David at the rectory, where she had her own room with its single bed and brightly flowered bed cover, in which she never slept, preferring instead to join David in the big double bed originally meant for him and Liz. Although David took a childish delight in using coarse words such as 'bum' and 'tits', and never tired of telling Rita how much he admired hers, they coupled together sparsely, enjoying it all the more on account of its speciality. Although Rita had written to Liz resigning her position and telling her of her new job, she had mentioned nothing about moving into the rectory and neither had David when talking to Liz over the phone. So it was that she caught the two of them in bed together in July of that year on one of her flying visits to Ashden. Upset at first, she soon came round to realising that Rita was a far more suitable partner for David than she could ever hope to be. Since child custody would not be a problem and financial arrangements were non existent on account of Liz earning far more than David, arranging a divorce on grounds of separation would not prove difficult. Better still, since Church of England canon law now allowed for clergy to remarry after divorce, there was no danger of David losing his job should he remarry as he fully intended to do. The irony of it all was that Liz was in the process of negotiating the purchase of a property in Bobbington. In the autumn she was taking up the offer of an important appointment at the University of East Anglia little more than twenty five miles away near Norwich, which meant she could commute by car on a daily basis. This meant that Jeremy and Anne would have a home there, besides which Jeremy would have another home with Roy and Verity at Rose Cottage and Anne a second home with David and Rita at the rectory.

As it turned out, Father David had been wrong to suppose that Liz would be having affairs with other men. The truth was that she truly loved him in her peculiar way and had loved having it off with him whenever she could find the time. For this reason she would sorely miss him, but there was always the Sisterhood, in which she planned to play a more active role now that she was going lived no more than a few miles from Lisa's Lodge. In any case, one sometimes simply had to love and let go; and, in this case, how could she possibly stand in the way of David's happiness in the arms of the buxom Rita?

It was sometime after these events that one night, as Father David and Rita lay close together in bed bathing in the afterglow of one of their infrequent sexual encounters, they fell into a discussion about human relationships. Although Father David had come to Ashden with strict beliefs concerning the sanctity of marriage, divorce, abortion and the rearing of children, events had since conspired to cause him to change his mind. The morality engendered by the beliefs of the Sisterhood not only worked well in practice, but also fostered compassionate attitudes in those who practised it. Although the standard form of husband/wife marriage was not always entered into by members of the Sisterhood, any children resulting from other forms of man/woman liaisons were reared to mature in an atmosphere of mutual caring and responsibility for one another's needs. Ashden was one of the few villages left where people placed need before nicety and motherliness before moral judgements. It was as if everyone had agreed to flout Christian convention in order to be closer to the true teaching of Jesus. After all, didn't he understand women - his mother, Martha and Mary and Mary Magdalene and all that? Would he not have rejoiced in beholding the love in their eyes, the beauty in their bodies and the sheen in their long, dark hair? Who knows? Maybe the real reason he was crucified was because he realised only too well the true value of womankind, and the chief men of his day were afraid that his teaching would lead to women taking over and robbing them of their power to rule. As time passed, maybe the early church leaders had deliberately obscured the important role Jesus had intended for women in the Church in case it would prove to be an insurmountable threat to male dominance. Who could now tell? All Father David knew was that the morality fostered by the Sisterhood in Ashden had been instrumental in bringing a shining light into his life in the shape of his beloved Rita, causing him to become an even better priest as a result.

And so the years passed and, as the Twentieth Century near its end, computers and mobile phones began to dominate life with ever increasing ferocity. Ashden struggled to maintain its individuality and the Sisterhood refused to give up the fight for matriarchal values in the face of ferocious male chauvinism aided and abetted by a host of female sycophants drunk on the dregs of patriarchal religious dogma. Older, including founder, members passed on and new members joined. Roy was nearing seventy with Verity not far behind, and both Parson Thurlow and his wife Flora had died. Emma settled happily into her new home at Kiln House and Liz reasonably happily into her new home in Bobbington. Jeremy, Anne, Oscar and Carol, now all grown up, had completed their education in one way or another and were all gainfully employed. Roy and Verity, Melanie and Moira all still lived in Bumber Close, Roy and Verity in Rose Cottage, Melanie in Briar Cottage and Moira in Mousehole Cottage. Neither Melanie nor Moira had married, although the former continued to enjoy occasional visits from Ted Mouser with Susan's blessing. As for Head Gardener Moira, she was far too enmeshed with the natural world around her to feel any need for a love life with any mere male. But all that was about to change with fascinating consequences.

Chapter 16

Moira

To everyone's surprise, Jane had decided to go and live with Coy Bateman in his farmhouse at Red House Farm, Felsham. Liking each other from the beginning, Coy and Oscar enjoyed something akin to a good father-son relationship, and Coy was minded to make him his heir. Having obtained a degree in Biology, Oscar was now working for the Royal Society for the Protection of Birds, and Coy had decided to farm organically. Respecting Jane's wish not to have any more children, he was more than happy for her to continue in her well paid job as estate manager on the Ashden Estate. However, he was less than happy that she had not, so far, agreed to marry him. He was certainly enjoying his cake, but he would have preferred it to have some icing on it.

On occasion Moira would turn up at Red House Farm in order to find out how its flora and fauna compared with those of Ashden. In particular, she was at pains to find out if any plants grew there that were not found on the Ashden Estate. Since the soil was heavier at Felsham, there was a distinct possibility that she would indeed find such plants. It was on one such visit that she met up with a strange lopsided, lolloping load of a fellow gangling his way along the high-hedged lane that ran along one side of Coy's land to where it connected with

Cooper's Copse, some twenty acres of coppiced woodland belonging to Red House Farm where it joined up with land belonging to another farm.

Coming to a shambling halt directly in front her, this scarecrow-like figure waved its arms around as if it were some kind of travelling windmill as it demanded to know what business she had to be walking on private land. Her amusement at being confronted with such an outlandish epitome of dishevelment overcoming any fear it might have instilled in her, Moira laughingly explained who she was.

The arm waving stopped and the scarecrow regarded her with some intensity for a moment or two before responding with: 'Oh; so yow be her sister then? I mean, her what live with Master Bateman.'

'That's right; and who might you be, if that's not a rude question?'

'Rude? Oh no, t'aint rude. I'm him what work for Master Bateman. Just the one he employ now, so he do. Tha's to say, employ all year round. He do often take on casuals at busy times.'

'Then, you must be the man they call Shoals? I've heard mention of you from Coy - Mr Bateman, I mean.'

'Well now, that's right. Shoals I answer to, but my real name is Fred - Fred Fairweather. And if you be her sister, then you must be her what garden up at Ashden Hall'

Moira's laughter rippled around the two of them as she responded with: 'You have it in nutshell! And now, would you mind if I turned back and went with you to wherever you're going?'

Seconds later found the two of them walking back along the lane together towards the farmhouse. Indulging in some surreptitious sniffs expecting to discover that her eccentric companion would give off some kind of sweaty-pissy smell tinged with tobacco, Moira was agreeably surprised to discover that he smelt quite fresh and clean. Presently she asked cheekily if he ever dressed up in his best clothes. Shoals didn't. He hadn't got any. He didn't have best and worst; his clothes were just clothes, any old thing, maybe, but clean, mended and enough to keep him both warm and decent. Moira supposed that his wife was kept busy patching them up. Wife? No, he didn't have a wife. Never had, in fact. His mother had died long ago and he'd lived alone since his father died some four years back. Always on the go, he was: farming, cooking, cleaning, mending, gardening - it was all grist that came to his mill. Life was there to be got on with, that was his motto. Had he never thought of marrying? No, he hadn't. Didn't think he'd make much of a father if they had kids. Besides, he wasn't keen on company. Preferred his own. That's to say, his own along with the wild things. He lived in an isolated cottage on the far side of Cooper's Copse. Women didn't want to live in places like that these days. Moira wondered if he'd ever had a girl friend. However, since he had been so obliging in answering her questions thus far, she didn't care to press him further. Anyway, by this time, they'd reached the farmhouse, where she bid him goodbye and went inside.

Jane was surprised to see her back so soon. Having explained what happened, Moira went on to ask if Shoals had ever had a girl friend. Jane didn't know. Moira would have to ask Coy. However, what she did know was that Shoals was known to visit Bessie Burton at Dorkings' Drift Cottage from time to time. Buxom Bessie, now in her fifties, had long been regarded as the local whore, although the title wasn't strictly true, she being very selective about whom she bedded. Having been left with a boy to bring up when her husband had died young, she had turned to taking in two or three well to do paying clients to supplement her meagre income. Shoals had been an afterthought. Never having charged him very much, she appreciated his attentions more than ever now that she was 'passed her best', so to speak. Although there were some who despised her, she was generally well liked, especially by the more affluent villagers, some of whom employed her to clean their houses. Since Moira had an inquisitive turn of mind, as her keen interest discovering all she could about the natural world around her showed, she was determined to find out more about the fascinating Shoals and his 'call girl' paramour.

Felsham was more hamlet than village consisting of a small cluster of dwellings around its tiny church, and it possessed neither post office nor shops of any kind. Beyond the village, the actual parish area was quite large containing a number of farmsteads and a few scattered cottages, originally built to house farm workers, but now mostly owned by well to do commuters and retired folk. In fact, Bessie Burton's dwelling, known as Pye's Cottage, and Shoal's home at Cooper's Cottage, were the only remaining out-of-village dwellings that had not been bought up in this way. Whereas Shoal's cottage still belonged to Red House Farm, Bessie had bought Pye's Cottage some years ago with her 'immoral' earnings before house prices had begun to rocket to their current levels. Pye's Cottage was situated down a short lane about half a mile out of the village on the road to Bobbington, and it was there that Moira found her one mellow Sunday afternoon in mid

September seated in her large back garden enjoying a cup of tea in the shade of an gnarled hawthorn tree.

Halfway across the ragged lawn, Moira hesitated, calling out in a timorous tone of voice: 'Hello there! Sorry to disturb you. I couldn't make anyone hear at the front door.'

Her beige trousered legs supported by one collapsible garden chair with her ample buttocks resting on another of similar design on the far side of a rickety old garden table, Bessie responded nonchalantly: 'Oh, it's you is it? I've been expecting you. Come over here, find yourself a chair and sit down.'

'Expecting me? I don't understand.' Her hand on a spare chair, Moira paused.

'Well, you're that gardener woman, aren't you? Shoals said you'd be paying me a visit. That's right. Sit yourself down. Would you like some tea?' She motioned towards the cosied teapot. 'Well, you needn't look so surprised! It maybe in a teapot, but it's made with tea bags.' As she leaned forward to reach for the teapot, her open necked, floral patterned blouse parted to reveal her deep cleavage.

Moira was disgusted. Used as she was to her own neat wee pair, she always regarded bit tits as being vulgar. Reaching for the proffered cup and saucer, she sipped bravely at the strong, stewed brew that passed for tea. How anyone could possibly prefer such tar when they could enjoy the soothing wetness of weak tea from a large mug was beyond her.

Suddenly, Bessie asked her how old she was. Contriving not to show her surprise at such directness, Moira nonchalantly replied that she was thirty five, at which information Bessie threw back her head and laughed loudly. 'Good for you! That should suit him just fine!'

'I don't understand. Suit whom?'

'Why, our Shoals of course! I mean, that's why you're here isn't it? Looking up about him to find out what kind of a tart he's been shagging with and all that?'

Refusing to be brow beaten and sitting her ground, Moira remained calm. 'As far as I know, he doesn't shag tarts; he eats them,' she responded quietly in a level tone of voice.

Bessie's roar of laugher, acting as a thawing agent, was also the catalyst enabling mutual respect. Moira asked for more information about Shoals and Bessie did her best to provide it. He was enigmatic in that, although he was a great adaptor, he was also, in essence, a throwback to an earlier age of rural isolation. In other words, he was a true countryman who, in an age of urban creep, had refused to surrender his rural heritage to the worldwide web even though he owned a computer that he could use along with the best of them. Being able to access horticultural information on websites and order seeds online simply gave him more spare time to live out his rural idyll, a way of life he was determined not to relinquish at any price. Hence his reluctance to marry. Most modern girls were far too townified for his liking. Hence his sudden liking for Moira. After his first meeting with her, he had raced on to Pye's Cottage to tell her all about it. Pleased for him, Bessie's only anxiety was that Moira might not reciprocate or, if she did, she might then be deterred by his long association with a woman of loose morals. Seeking to reassure her on that point, Moira ventured the opinion that morals were worthless unless they could be adapted to circumstance. Since Bessie had had a moral duty to care for her son and give him as good a start in life as possible, was it then immoral for her to provide above average sustenance for him by entertaining wealthy clients in her bed? Having once fallen for an unwanted pregnancy, she wasn't going to make the same mistake twice, but simply provide a first rate service to men who felt the need for that something extra they weren't getting from their wives.

It wasn't always that some men stopped caring for their wives; their love for them often led them to respect them in ways that precluded too much variation in their sexual encounters. It wasn't even that such men were over-bothered with wanting sex; they simply sometimes needed relief for a powerful urge. Understanding all of this, Moira also realised Bessie's coarse turn of speech and laissez faire attitude were little more than a smokescreen raised by her to conceal a caring personality. Not only had she done the best for her son in the only way she knew how, she had also given emotional support to Shoals and brought him relief in a rapidly changing world, in which he found it difficult to find a mate in tune with his values. But Moira's visit signalled the end of all this. If she hadn't been keen on Shoals she wouldn't have bothered to call on his whore woman. That being so, suffice it to say that Moira and Bessie parted firm friends with Moira knowing precisely what she had to do.

The following Sunday morning Shoals made no attempt too conceal his pleasure when Moira called to see him at Cooper's Cottage. Accepting his offer to come inside, she was agreeably surprised at how clean and neat he kept his kitchen, where he had taken her, saying it was cosier in there, although they could go into the front room if she preferred, which Moira didn't. What she had to say could just as well be said in the kitchen. Accepting his offer of a cup of coffee, she dissuaded him from beginning to make it right away.

'There's something I want to ask you first,' she said, her eyes twinkling.

'Fire away then, gal!'

'Will you marry me?'

The beginnings of a grin flickering around the corner of Shoal's lips gradually spread across them and from there to his whole face before erupting into a loud laugh that was more like a cry of joy. 'I thought you'd never ask!'

Throwing her arms around him, Moira hugged him to her. Responding in like kind, he said: 'I wanted it to be you who asked me. I like it that way.'

Moira kissed him. 'So do I! And while we're at it, I want neither church wedding nor wedding ring. What I do, I do of my own freewill and I'll wear no band as a symbol that I'm bound to any man.'

Shoals loosened his hold. 'I'll make you that coffee,' he said.

Moira sat down at the kitchen table. 'There's another thing: there'll be no sex before marriage. I want us to do all of it our way and not be bound by any kind of convention.'

Setting a large mug of coffee before her, Shoals agreed, adding: 'And children? Are we to have children?'

Moira nodded. 'If at all possible, yes. That's to say, **child**. I'm a little on the old side for more than that, but one, yes - all being well. I'll come to an arrangement with Lord Denver to enable me to keep my job as head gardener at the hall. But we need to get on with it. I'll contact the registry office tomorrow.'

Coming to kneel by her chair, Shoals enfolded her once again in his arms. 'You're my kind of woman - the kind I've looked for this passed twenty years or more and thought I'd never find,' he said.

As things turned out there was a double wedding a few days before Christmas when Moira married Shoals and Jane married Coy, and no one was more delighted than Roy at the way things had turned out.

Chapter 17

Roy

The years passed, Roy was now well into his seventies and the Sisterhood continued to thrive. Apart from six months maternity leave, the arrival of Moira's son, Roy Frederick, had had little impact on her position as head gardener at Ashden Hall. When he was very small she took him to work with her in his pram, stopping to breast feed him, change his nappies and so on whenever needed. Then, when he began to walk, she would take him round the gardens with her. Since she was mainly supervising and organising it was easier to cope with the child than it would have been had she been doing the actual manual work. Later, after he began to attend nursery school, it was even easier for her to cope. Lord Denver had been most accommodating, allowing her time off whenever she needed it without any deductions in salary. Susan, the one time nanny now wed to Ted Mouser and living with him at Elm Farm, Teddlethwaite, had been keen to help, always happy to look after the young Roy for a reasonable remuneration whenever needed. Shoals was a as devoted a father as he was husband, and he and Moira had taken out a mortgage on Cooper's Cottage, which Coy and Jane had agreed to sell them. Bessie Burton, now styled 'Auntie Bessie', also did her turn at caring for the young Roy. Although Moira fancied that Shoals now and then indulged in 'a bit on the side' with her, she minded not at all. It was hardly fair to expect him to give up on such a long standing arrangement. In any case, it fascinated her that Bessie, now over sixty, was still capable of enjoying herself in that way. Not over keen on too much sexual activity, Moira would much rather rejoice in Shoal's overwhelming love for her as she actually was and not just because he saw her as an attractive female there to satisfy his sexual needs.

Under Melanie's leadership, the Sisterhood had adapted to meet the challenges of the Twenty First Century, its main aim now being to foster the chances of women being appointed into positions of influence and control in all walks of society whilst, at the same time, doing everything possible to encourage matriarchy throughout society in general. Although it was uphill work, the Sisterhood could claim several notable successes. Although Faith's adventure into group parentage as tried out in Bumber Close was ongoing in other places, emphasis was now being placed on encouraging women to take control in more normal marriage scenarios. In this respect, Moira's teaming up with Shoals was much appreciated. Never an ardent member of the Sisterhood, Moira had since proved her worth by showing that a comparative loner such as herself could, nevertheless, play a vital roll in working for a more equitable future for everyone. Since most religions placed too much emphasis on their followers adhering to a 'one size fits all' kind of morality, the Sisterhood was at pains to bring about a more naturally fluid type of morality geared to need rather than to arbitrary rules. Circumstances altered cases. What was right in one instance could easily be wrong in another and vice-versa. Whilst it might be generally true that children fared best when reared in a congenially affluent husband-wife, mother-father family atmosphere, this wasn't always the case. It was always a matter of using something that worked rather than working something that was useless. Too much of what passed for morality was all about squeezing people into moulds that didn't fit them. If water could find its own level, so could morality. Blanket morality inevitably ended up as brutality. Melanie was sure of that.

Father David, having agreed an amicable divorce with Liz, was now happily married to Rita with both of them now well into middle age. Roy would sometimes pop in to see them, when they would discuss old times and he would tell them about Faith, Charity, Flora and Parson Thurlow. Although fewer people now attended church, the attendance at Saint Mary's, Ashden still remained well above the national average, the reason for this being, according to Roy, that Father David had followed in Parson Thurlow's footsteps by emphasising compassion in the context of a flexible morality in preference to adopting 'a one size fits all' attitude. Remembering his escapades with Liz and Rita's rescue of him, Father David had little choice but to agree with this analysis. Happily for him, his daughter Anne was now spending more time at the rectory than she was with her mother Liz in her new home at Bobbington. Having been nannied by Rita, Anne regarded her as a mother figure, relating better to her than she did to her natural mother.

Roy had taken to visiting Emma, now long since happily ensconced in Kiln Cottage, on a regular basis, the two of them having become firm friends. Having got to know Emma better through their mutual membership of the Sisterhood, Verity's animosity towards her had long since evaporated, which meant that she was happy for Roy to be friends with her. Emma once told Roy that he had an original mind. His thought patterns were almost totally devoid of the clichéd platitudes doing the rounds in the majority of minds. Although he rarely left the village, even for an annual holiday break, he often knew more about other lands than many of those who spent their holidays in them.

Kiln Cottage was redolent with nostalgia for Roy, who could never go there without recalling some event from the past involving Faith, Charity and himself. He would sit in the front room, look around him and visualise how the furniture had been arranged when the sisters lived there; but he never mentioned any of this to Emma. It was one bleak autumn afternoon when he called in to see her, after he had been visiting her in this fashion for some years, that she suddenly asked him if he had ever regretted never having made love to her.

Roy shook his head. 'No, not at all. The way I see it, close relationships between men and women don't always have to involve sex. The way I see it is that it can ruin a relationship. Looking around me, I see far too many people entering into relationships looking for sex rather than just letting it happen if it's going to. But then, maybe I'm not the best person to ask about such matters. Fact is, in my teens I was never much interested in running after girls. You see, it was Faith; she just chose me and it all happened that way. She sort of - well, she schooled me into, if you see what I mean.'

Assuring him that she did, Emma added: 'You've never had to look for sex, have you? I mean, it's always - well, sort of - come to you?'

Roy nodded. 'That's right. I've never run after women; they've come to me; and sexual intercourse never happened unless they wanted it.'

Emma's eyebrows moved upwards ever so slightly. 'Are you saying that you've never wanted to do it badly with any woman without her not wanting to do it with you first?'

Roy shook his head. 'Oh no, I didn't mean that. You see, it's like this: it all began with Faith when she kissed me under the mistletoe. It was the sheer closeness of her, like as if she'd enveloped me into a whole new, thrilling world of mystery and imagination, in which the mystery and the imagination were both real - if you see what I mean. I know it's contradictory, but that's how it was. Even now, after all this time, I can vividly recall the womanly smell of her - of how I breathed it all in and opened my mouth to her as she pressed her lips to mine and we joined together in that long, deep, lingering kiss, and of how I ran my hands over her thighs and buttocks, thrilling to the firm, round smoothness of them, and wanting to hold onto to them forever like as if I'd just discovered something overwhelmingly precious. Indeed yes, of course I wanted her again and again, and that's why I avoided her for weeks with all that display of boyish shyness. Then, the night of the great snow storm, when she came into the bedroom and stripped off in front of me, I was in my seventh heaven - and even beyond that when we coupled up together. Faith taught me the way, and ever since then I've waited for women to come to me, and they have, each in her own way. Some I've wanted and some I haven't; but I've tried to fit in with what each and everyone of them wanted of me, and I have few regrets.'

Emma smiled knowingly. 'Regrets? There were some, then, that you would rather not have coupled with, and maybe some, or just someone, you would have liked to have had it off with, if you'll excuse my choice of words, but never did?'

Roy chuckled. 'We need to get a few things straight here.

We're talking as if I'd lain with dozens of women when, in actual fact, I've done it with just five, two of whom I'd really rather not have obliged in that way.'

'And are you going to tell me who they are?'

Roy nodded slowly. 'Oh yes; there's no secret about it. You may have already guessed: Liz and Melanie.'

'And you didn't enjoy it with them?'

'Oh, I didn't say that! I had little choice. They choose me; I did as I was told and entered into the spirit of the thing - just as I was supposed to. At least, I **supposed** that to be the case. Without a fair dose of supposition life would be dull indeed. Leastways, that's how I see it.'

Emma laughed her appreciation of Roy's reasoning. 'And the other three? Faith, Charity and Verity, I assume?'

Roy nodded. 'That's right. But here again it was a case of them choosing me and not I them. It's as if I'd discovered an enchanted landscape into which I then merged to discover the real world, in which I could be true to myself. Many people are not happy because they're not true to themselves; their life is a pretence, which they mistake for reality. Worse still, too many people are bound by their beliefs when they should be liberated by them. Too much emphasis is based on **what** we do, when it should be on **how** we do things. No one has to pursue happiness; it's already there inside us; all we have to do is to recognise it.'

Emma sighed. 'You know more of life than those of us who've travelled widely. Although, I have to say, I'm glad I was able to spend some time in the Congo with the bonobos.'

Roy's eyes twinkled. 'And you think I'm a bit like them?'

Emma shook her head. 'Not you, Roy. At least not you alone. It's the Sisterhood who've followed the bonobo trail and taken you along with them. And the amazing thing is: it's actually worked!'

Now in her mid seventies, Emma was still a striking figure of a woman, with her now grey hair tumbling about her shoulders as one might expect to see it in a young girl. Liking women as he did and friends with many, he was well aware of the value of such non-sexual relationships, amongst which the judged his friendship with Emma to be paramount. Only his friendship with Melanie was deeper, but then, he had coupled with her once, as part of a solemn ritual it was true, but coupled nevertheless. Conversely, his fathering of Jeremy with Liz had not improved his relationship with her. Friendship wasn't the problem. They liked each other well enough in that way. It was simply that he found her temperament to be too volcanic for him to feel comfortable with for too long. Although he loved Jeremy as much as any of his children, he still tended to feel that what had happened between Liz and himself had been a mistake. He shouldn't have allowed Verity to persuade him that it was all right. But then again, who was he to argue? The Sisterhood had decided and he had obeyed. The result was that he and Liz now had a son of whom both of them could be justly proud. Since it was women who bore babies, it seemed only right to him that they should have full control over if, how, when and where they should have them. So, since Jeremy himself was certainly not a 'mistake', he accepted what had happened without rancour.

That same evening, as Roy and Verity sat by the fire in Rose Cottage, he mentioned Dan, wondering what would have happened had he lived into old age.

Verity didn't doubt that she would have managed. 'I enjoyed having two husbands,' she said. 'It was a challenge, certainly; but I like to think that I coped with it well. The main thing was, it worked. Dan was happy about you and me and he and you were good friends. So what's the problem?'

Nodding his acceptance of this analysis, Roy said that he had to accept that there wasn't one. He had wondered, that was all, just as one wondered about lots of things. Such as Emma, for instance. Although, on the face of it, he had come to know her well, she remained something of an enigma to him; there was still that something about her he had never quite fathomed.

Verity looked into the fire. 'I might be able to help there,' she said in a distant tone of voice. 'But not now. It's getting late. Besides, there's someone else we need to see first.'

Cuddling up to Verity in bed that night, Roy thought how this was the most meaningful thing of all in any man-woman relationship. After all, actual sexual encounters formed no more than a tiny part of one's life. Thanks to Faith and Charity he had learned to get such matters into perspective at an early age. In his relationship with Faith, it was just her being there and knowing he could discuss anything with her that was truly important with her providing sexual treats for him only when she knew he needed them. Through her he had learned the ways of the female mind, enabling him to relate so well to most women folk without needing to see them as sex objects. He had never needed to seek sex; the women who had wanted it with him had sought him out and asked him; and he was glad for that. Although he still couldn't truly imagine what things would have been like had Dan lived longer, he earnestly believed that Verity would have found a way to make it all work out well.

Early the following afternoon, Roy followed Verity out into the back garden at Rose Cottage at her bidding. With autumn now well advanced, everywhere was carpeted with leaves including the bear cave Roy had made for Dan's daughter Jane. He had kept it for the grandchildren when they came to visit, and the swing and other playthings were also still there. Roy had always been good with children and all his grandchildren loved him. Placing an arm around him, Verity cuddled up to his side. After a few moments, she told him that she was expecting a visitor any minute.

'And now she tells me!' Roy's tone of voice was playful. 'And are you going to tell me who it is?'

'Oh… Someone you know - well, in fact. She's one of your paramours.'

'My paramours? You're talking as if I had dozens of them!'

Verity giggled. 'And so you might have for all I know! But seriously, this one is special - a one off, you might say. There! If I'm not mistaken, that's the door bell.'

Back indoors, Roy waited in the front room whilst Verity answered the door. Seconds later, she ushered Melanie into his presence. Roy made no attempt to hide his surprise. She was the last person he had expected to see.

'I've come to tell you something you really ought to have been told long ago,' she said after they were all seated.

'And it's about Emma, isn't it?' Roy said looking straight at her.

Melanie nodded. 'That's right. And as head of the Sisterhood it's my job to set the record straight. Although Emma liked you a lot from the first moment you met each other, when Faith realised that there was never going to be any risk of sexual relations developing between you, she decided not to saddle Emma with the true facts concerning her parentage. It was enough that she had found her natural mother without burdening her with details concerning her natural father, who had died less than five years after her birth. As much as anything, he'd been the reason why Charity had not been allowed to keep the baby.'

Roy leaned forward. 'And was he someone I would've known?'

Melanie nodded. 'He was your grandfather. That's to say, your father's father. Charity and he had an affair. Since it wasn't under the auspices of the Sisterhood, which didn't even exist in those days, it was a rather sleazy business. She told me about it not long before she died, saying for me to keep it to myself unless there came a time when I thought it relevant to divulge what I knew to any interested party. As I'd taken Faith's place as head of the Sisterhood, she thought I was the right person to have knowledge of such matters.'

Not altogether surprised, Roy nodded his understanding. Having been around seven when his grandfather had died, Roy remembered him rather vaguely as an austere, if vaguely comic, figure with a large, bushy moustache. 'Let me see now,' he said. 'That would make Emma into a sort of aunt of mind, wouldn't it?' The thought of this amusing him somewhat, he laughed a little before adding: 'And are you going to tell her what you've told me?'

Melanie shook her head. 'No: that's to say, not unless she begins to try and find out for herself. So far, she's been content with finding her real mother. Verity assessed that the time had arrived when you needed to know. However, as I see it, it looks as if Emma may never need to know.'

Standing up, Roy reached out with his hands, one for each woman. 'Come! Let's return to the garden. It's a lovely day for the time of the year and I want to show you something.'

Outside again, Roy pointed towards the bear cave. 'It represents the womb,' he said. 'And it's an epitome of the universe, which is like a vast womb perpetually nurturing and perpetually giving birth. We all come from the womb and, when we die, it's like we're returning to the womb. The womb is sacred. We should treat it with the utmost respect. Problems begin when a male dominated world insists on treating the womb as a nurturing place for the perpetuation of male power. In Ashden things are different because, here, the womb has taken control, women are calling the tune and men have found happiness in following their creative lead. Men are at their best when their creativity stems from womb power. Using the womb as a breeding place for male egoism always spells disaster.'

Roy's eloquence was something else he'd learnt from Faith, and the two women knew that. Presently, Melanie asked him what had truly been the greatest influence on his life, and neither she nor Verity were surprised when he told them that it was the landscape. It shapes us all, and the only sure way to survive happily is to adapt to it. When we failed to do this we were helping to destroy the planet. Human activities such as farming and gardening were at their best when they fitted in with the landscape. He liked to think he'd fitted in with the landscape, and he'd also fitted in with women because they were like a landscape to him, and it had all begun with Faith when he'd explored the landscape of her body under the mistletoe.

Slowly they turned and went inside again, back into the front room, where Roy and Melanie seated themselves together on the long sofa, leaving room for Verity when she returned to them with afternoon tea. Then, after tea, when the three of them were seated together with Roy in the middle, the women cuddled closer, Verity with her head on one shoulder and Melanie with hers on the other.

Verity sighed. 'Oh… Melanie… What shall we do with him?'

Melanie kissed him on the cheek. 'I dunno… Just try to keep him safe, like we've always done, I shouldn't wonder… 'Cos, when he's gone, goodness knows who'll we get to replace him!'

Roy took a deep breath and then chuckled. 'Try Shoals,' he said. 'He'll keep things ticking over until… until…'

'Until what, Roy?' the two women echoed together.

'Until Moira's wee Roy's old enough to take over, that's what.'

After that, they took him upstairs and laid him on the bed, where he presently went to sleep in the arms of the Sisterhood.

The End

Lightning Source UK Ltd.
Milton Keynes UK
05 October 2009

144550UK00001B/8/P